THE AAYAKUDI MURDERS

by Indra Soundar Rajan

translated by Nirmal Rajagopalan

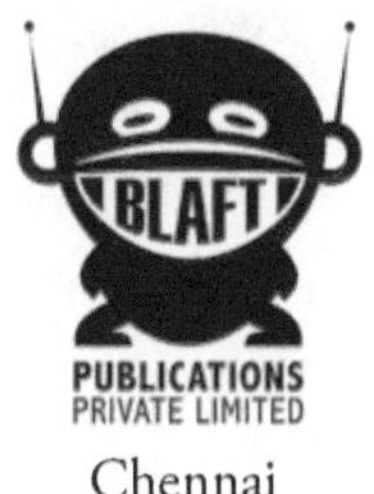

BLAFT
PUBLICATIONS
PRIVATE LIMITED
Chennai

Published in India in 2019 by
Blaft Publications Pvt. Ltd.

ISBN 978 93 80636 33 7

This project was supported by a grant from the Shuttleworth Foundation.

Blaft Publications Pvt. Ltd.
4/192 Ellaiamman Koil St.
Neelankarai
Chennai 600041
www.blaft.com

THE
AAYAKUDI
MURDERS

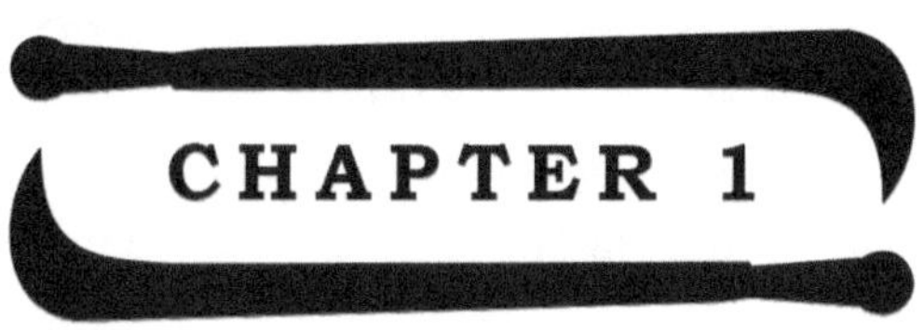

CHAPTER 1

It was June. Ash-coloured rain clouds had set up camp across the Chennai sky. Rajendran looked up at them as he kick-started his TVS Victor, hoping that they would stay still rather than scatter. The leather strap of his bag was slung across his shoulder; within the bag was the tomato rice his mother had prepared for his lunch. The fragrant aroma escaped the bag, wafted through the air in search of his nose, and floated inside.

"Amma is amma only!" he said to himself.

The bike started with the first kick.

Bikes are better suited than cars for the busy roads of Chennai. You can squeeze through tiny gaps between the vehicles and keep moving forward—which was just what Rajendran did.

He had to be in his seat in the office by ten o'clock. It was a big responsibility, the job of a reporter. Piled on his table was a mountain of papers, letters, stories, and poems. He had to read through them all carefully and select the most interesting ones. Apart from that, he had to find time to visit the local big shots and interview them. There were many incidents that tested his patience, but he had to always keep his cool. If he let his emotions get the better of him, a good story lead could fall apart, like a rolling egg cracking open on the floor.

His senior editor had told him that there was an important meeting that morning. Rajendran had enough experience to know that when his boss called for a meeting like that, it meant that he had hooked a big fish—maybe even an eel.

As he raced through the traffic, Rajendran wondered what it could all be about. His youth made him fearless, and the bike travelled fast. He usually got to his seat within ten minutes of leaving home. The office was four kilometres away; in those four kilometres there were four traffic signals. He crossed all of them, and within ten minutes he rode past the signboard of Tamil Nadu's famous investigative weekly, *Selvam*. He parked the Victor, adjusted his leather bag, and entered the office.

On his desk was a small piece of paper. *Meet the editor immediately*, the note read. He knew the handwriting; it belonged to the editor's assistant, Banumathi. He carefully placed his leather bag in a corner under his desk and left at once.

It was a big printing press, one that produced lakhs of copies of various magazines. As he walked through the office, the unpleasant smell of ink followed him, making him wrinkle his nose. Simultaneously, the cool blast from the A/Cs chilled his skin.

He stopped in front of the editor's cabin, opened the door, and said, "Good morning, sir."

Inside, the editor was deep in thought. "Very good morning. Come in," he said, and signalled to Rajendran to be seated.

"Yes, sir?"

"An important assignment, Rajendran."

"Great, sir. Tell me."

"Do you believe in ghosts? Demons?"

What an opening question! Rajendran sat up, surprised. "What's this about, sir?" he asked.

"Give me an answer first."

"No, sir."

"Good, we're on the same page then. A girl from a village called Aayakudi has sent us a letter about some unbelievable occurrences taking place there. She has written that, according to the village folk, it's the work of a *kaathu karuppu*—an evil spirit."

Rajendran laughed sarcastically.

"What? Why are you laughing?"

"What else to do other than laugh? Such superstitions are fairly common in villages."

"That may be. But how often does a village girl write to a magazine office asking them to come and uncover the truth?"

"You're right, sir, it's interesting. Who's the girl?"

"Her name is Chinna Pechi. Look at this handwriting; it's as beautiful as a string of pearls. I'd say she's definitely either completed high school, or she's about to. Have a look."

Rajendran picked up the letter and began reading.

Vanakkam Editor,

I am an avid reader of your magazine. In our village, there is a Tamil teacher by the name of Deenadayalan. I have read back issues of Selvam *at his house.*

I truly believe that Selvam *is a great asset for us readers. From tearing off the masks of politicians to revealing the activities of fake godmen,* Selvam *is always there on the front lines.*

I am from a farming family. My father, Ramasamy, is a goatherd. Sometimes I go with him when he takes the animals to graze. Near our village there is a rocky hill where we take the cattle and goats. Lately, though, the animals are scared go near there. My father has been bedridden for a few days, and we suspect that he saw something he shouldn't have.

Once, a goat did not return to the flock. I went looking for it, when suddenly the ground started shaking right beneath my feet.

Nothing like this had ever happened to me before; it was all new and strange.

When I told some people in our village about it, they said that it was the work of the ghosts who inhabit that place. That's what my father believes too. I, however, am doubtful. I think there's something else going on, some sort of criminal activity. One day I saw a man dressed in prison clothes hiding in the sugarcane field. As soon as he saw me looking at him, he ran towards the hill. I think he is up to something out there.

I am scared to tell the police about all this. Illicit country liquor is being sold in my village, and I have seen the police take money from the people who sell the liquor instead of apprehending them. That's why I am hesitant to go to the authorities.

In my mind, your magazine serves as a forum for justice. On reading this letter, please do what you have to. I am ready to help in whatever way I can.

Sincerely,
Chinna Pechi

Rajendran arched his eyebrows in surprise.

"So? What do you say now?"

"It's quite fascinating. It also makes me happy, sir, that this village girl considers our magazine to be a forum for justice! That's a big deal!"

"Absolutely! So, start for the village then. Show me your C.I.D. work."

"I'll leave right away, sir. It sounds to me like it's probably an escaped convict who's behind it."

"I think so too. But you should take some safety precautions. That village falls under Tirunelveli district; the Superintendent of Police there is a straightforward fellow. He has supported our magazine many times. Just drop in on him for a visit."

"Right, sir. I'll take care of it," said Rajendran, standing up.

The editor held out his hand. Rajendran reciprocated with a hearty handshake.

"Be careful. My personal cell phone will be on at all times if you need me."

Rajendran left with a smile.

* * *

The signboard reading AAYAKUDI, its paint cracked and peeling, stood in the middle of a clump of overgrown bushes.

CLICK!

That was first thing Rajendran collected in his camera. Flanking the board was a long dirt road, dotted with pits and bumps. The previous day's rainwater had turned the pits into pools of reddish gravy. A few frogs were using them as personal swimming pools, practicing their backstroke.

On either side of the dirt road, some shrubs had sprung up of their own volition, growing green and robust, with a few parthenium plants among them. Rajendran gazed at them as he walked.

Ahead, an old man leading two cows approached. He gave Rajendran's jeans and T-shirt a curious look.

"Who are you?" he asked, in the rural dialect.

"Just a person," replied Rajendran teasingly.

"See here! I only asked because you don't look like you're from around here."

"I'm a distant relative of Ramasamy's family," said Rajendran, quickly recalling the name from the letter.

"Which Ramasamy?" the old man asked, scratching his chin.

"Chinna Pechi's father."

"Ah, him! He's been laid out for more than a week. He refused to listen to anybody and took his animals out to graze by the hill—the evil spirit gave him one slap and laid him flat. Go, go and see him. No man can survive the touch of the spirit. Ramasamy's time is coming to an end any moment now."

He turned back to the cows, saying, "Hey, go! Hurrr!" and moved on.

Having picked up a few more nuggets of information from this brief conversation, Rajendran walked on slowly. After stopping to ask for directions from passers-by, he reached Ramasamy's hut.

There, another couple of shocks awaited. Ramasamy's corpse was there to welcome him. Crying by her father's feet was a girl, not more than eight or nine years old.

Could this little girl be the one who wrote such a detailed letter to the magazine?

As Rajendran stood there confused, grappling with the question, he was noticed by some of Ramasamy's relatives who had gathered at his home.

They came up to him. "Who are you, *thambi*?" one of them asked.

"Which one is Chinna Pechi…?"

"There, the one crying. That's the girl."

"Really? Her?"

"Yes, her. Why are you asking?"

"Well… Can you tell me how her father died?"

"Who are you, anyway? Why are you asking all these things?"

"I… um… let's just say I'm a distant relative. Pechi sent me a letter saying that her father was unwell."

"What? *This* girl sent you a letter?"

"You did say she's Chinna Pechi, right?"

"What are you talking about! You say you're a relative, but you don't seem to know anything at all! That girl is illiterate! She's never gone near a classroom, not even to seek shelter from the rain. How is she supposed to have written you a letter?"

Their cross questioning hit Rajendran squarely between the brows.

It's going to be tough to handle this crowd, Rajendran thought. Confused, he wondered where he'd gone wrong.

In the middle of all this, Chinna Pechi turned to look at him too. At first, she just gazed at him through her tears. Then she stepped closer and stared.

"Oh, so you've come?" she said… in the deep, bass voice of a man.

Rajendran stepped back, startled.

CHAPTER 2

RAJENDRAN STARED AT CHINNA PECHI in disbelief. He was certain his ears had heard a male voice coming from her. But abruptly, she switched back to her childish wail of "*Appa! Appa!*"

It seemed to Rajendran that just for a few seconds the girl had undergone some sort of transformation. As he stood there watching, someone pulled Chinna Pechi aside, pointed to Rajendran and asked "Do you know that man?" In response, Chinna Pechi simply stared at Rajendran, as one stares at a stranger.

An uneasy feeling came over Rajendran, as if ants were crawling all over him.

The person who had questioned Chinna Pechi now approached him. "Who are you, thambi? The girl doesn't seem to know you. How are you related to Ramasamy?"

"*Aiyya*, I am no relation. But my father knew Ramasamy. How he knew him, how well he knew him, I'm not really sure. When I heard that an evil spirit had attacked him, I couldn't believe it. I came to see him as soon as I heard the news," Rajendran improvised smoothly.

"Ah! Well that makes more sense. I was born and raised in this village. Ramasamy and I are about the same age; we grew up together. I'd see him every day, right from when we'd wash our feet at the pond in the morning until the time we went to sleep. I wondered how he could have suddenly ended up with a relative from the city without my knowing about it! By the way, are you Tirunelveli Ratnasamy's son?"

"Ratnasamy?"

"Yes. Ramasamy used to travel to Tirunelveli now and then. He told me he knew someone named Ratnasamy."

"That's right! I wondered how you knew my father's name," Rajendran said. The man nodded. It seemed that Rajendran had somehow managed to survive the interrogation.

Meanwhile, the village women, having let their hair loose, were shaking their heads about and wailing loudly, "*Maamoi!* You've left us!" The sound of their lamentations filled his ears.

Now and then, Pechi would look over and give him a piercing stare.

"Do you really think it was an evil spirit that struck him down?" Rajendran asked the man.

"Why, you don't believe it? That's your city schooling, teaching you to be sceptical of everything. Even when it's right in front of your eyes, you'll try to see it in a different way!"

"Don't get angry. I just asked so I could understand."

"If you're so curious, why bother asking me? Why don't you go take a walk over by the hill and the canal bank? Then you'll come to know everything by yourself. You won't have to take my word for it."

With that answer, the man wiped his face with the dirty towel he was carrying and walked away.

Puzzled, Rajendran turned back to look at Ramasamy's body. Then his gaze shifted again to Chinna Pechi. She was sobbing like a child who'd been separated from her parents at a crowded village fair.

Some people brought out a woman from within the hut, supporting her with their arms. The woman looked completely exhausted. As soon as she saw her, Chinna Pechi cried out "Amma!", wrapped her arms around the woman's hips, and continued to sob. Rajendran gathered at once that this woman was the dead Ramasamy's wife.

He retreated a bit from the miserable scene and stood at a distance. His cell phone started to ring in his waist pouch. He took it out and held it to his ear. It was his editor on the other end.

"Rajendran."

"Tell me, sir."

"Have you reached Aayakudi?"

"Yes sir, I'm here."

"What's that wailing sound?"

"There's been a new development. That girl who wrote us the letter—her father is dead. Everyone here says that the evil spirit struck him down."

"My God! Did you see the girl?"

"Yes, and here's the funny thing… She can't be more than eight years old, and she doesn't know how to read or write!"

"Then who wrote that letter?"

"I'll have to find that out, sir. But whoever wrote it, at least some of what it says is true. I got one of the villagers to talk to me for a bit and he said that if I went near the hill, I would learn about the spirit myself."

"So, what's your plan?"

"There's lots of work to be done, sir. But right now, I'm a little confused about which direction to head in first."

"The letter mentioned a Tamil teacher who reads our magazine."

"Oh, so you think that's the best path to take? Maybe you're right; if I meet him, that should help me get somewhere."

"Whatever you do, be careful. We're not the police department! I don't want to have to answer to your family if anything happens to you."

"Are you afraid for me, or warning me?"

"Both."

"What, you think I should come back? Why are you trying to talk me out of doing my job now?"

"If it were a straightforward criminal matter, I'd say go right ahead; it should be like eating halva for you. But this is different."

"A life has been lost, and they believe that this evil spirit is responsible. No one even seems to have an iota of doubt. And there are no police to be seen. We need to do something about it!"

"I can tell you feel strongly about it. Just be cautious when make your moves. And keep me updated. If you need anything, don't hesitate to ask."

"I won't have to ask, sir."

"Then?"

"You know me, sir. If I need anything, I'll just take it—you won't find me waiting for permission." With that, Rajendran cut the call.

He looked up. The crowd in front of him had grown. A garland of roses, as long as a man is tall, had been hung over a wooden frame that was being carried forward by two men with a small entourage behind them.

One of these men wore a muslin jibba, with slippers made of tire rubber on his feet. He sported a sharp moustache with the tips turned upwards. He looked every inch like a hero from an epic. His name, though Rajendran didn't know it yet, was Govinda Naicker.

The man at his side was Rajamanickam, Naicker's wife's brother. On Rajamanickam's cheek was a scar that looked like a sleeping centipede. If you looked at his face once, that was more than enough—it would stick in your memory forever. His eyes were very sharp.

Rajamanickam noticed Rajendran standing off to one side. *Who's this outsider?* his eyes wondered. He turned to one of the people next to him, silently relaying the question. That man, too, looked at Rajendran, measuring him up. He pursed his lips, turned back to Rajamanickam, and shook his head.

Rajendran observed it all. He caught hold of a person standing nearby and enquired, "Who are those two? They made quite an entrance!"

"Who are *you?* You must be new to the village."

"Yes."

"That's why you don't know Naicker. Naicker is the *naataamai*, the village headman—the panchayat president."

"Even in this day and age, you still use titles like 'naataamai'?"

"Oh, people with titles like that will be around as long as there *is* a village. Half the land in Aayakudi belongs to him. He's a very good man. The deceased, Ramasamy, used to work for him for a while. Because of that association he's come to offer his condolences."

"Who's that other man with him? Staring like a bird of prey!"

"Go on! Nice way of asking! If it happened to fall on his ears, he'd skin you like a goat! That's Rajamanickam, Naicker's brother-in-law. He's going to marry Naicker's daughter Thenmozhi, and then become his son-in-law too."

Nine answers for one question! thought Rajendran as he noted everything down in his mind.

Suddenly, the chorus of mourners raised the pitch of their crying. Ramasamy's wife buried her face into Naicker's chest and sobbed loudly. Rajamanickam lifted the white veshti that covered Ramasamy's body and peered at his chest. The skin over a large area was discoloured, dark with clotted blood.

"Looks like he saw the spirit face to face… A punch to the chest and he just collapsed and fell. He hasn't been able to speak for days. Before he died, he started foaming at the mouth," explained someone who was standing close by.

Rajamanickam considered this carefully, scratching his jaw.

Suddenly, to the astonishment of those standing near her, Chinna Pechi looked straight at Rajamanickam and fixed him with a powerful stare.

"Look here! The spirit has touched the girl now too," said the same man who had spoken before. "See how she stares at you like a *pey* every now and then." He pointed out Chinna Pechi to Rajamanickam, who turned to look at her. In that instant Chinna Pechi leaped straight onto

Rajamanickam and gripped him tight, like a monitor lizard gripping a sheer wall.

Several people joined together in prying her off. Rajamanickam looked shaken. Even Naicker was unnerved.

"Hey *aatha*, get the exorcist to come and look at the girl! You can't just leave things like this!" said a voice from the crowd.

Rajendran stood watching, fascinated.

At that moment, a thin older man came up to his side. "Vanakkam, thambi," he said. There was a gentleness in his hesitant voice.

"Vanakkam. And you are…?"

"I am the person you came here to meet. The Tamil teacher. Deenadayalan."

"Oh! So you're the one! How did you know who I was?"

"You stand out in this crowd. And besides, there's no chance of any other outsiders visiting this place. That's why I approached you so confidently."

"Very good! In the letter we received, there was a line about you."

"I know. I'm the one who wrote it."

"Really!" said Rajendran, surprised.

"I wrote it under Chinna Pechi's name. I could have used my own, but I had an idea that a letter written by a little girl would be sure to get noticed by your magazine, and that you would give it higher priority. Otherwise you would have treated it the same as an average reader's letter. And indeed, it seems to have done the trick; here you are!"

"What, sir! That's quite a twist! Anyway, let it be. What do you think of this death?"

"You'll have to go up that hill to find out the answer. If you want, I will help you."

"Do you think it's possible he was murdered? What could the motive be?"

"In my opinion, this is most likely the work of that escaped prisoner. Up on the hill, there are many caves; once you go inside it's hard to find your way out. Sometimes packs of jackals gather there. We even see leopards once in a while."

"So, you're convinced the convict is behind all of this?"

"What else to make of it? At the same time, seeing the way Pechi is behaving—a few thoughts have occurred to me…"

"What sort of thoughts?"

The teacher looked back at the mourners. "We don't have to stand here and talk. Let's go over there."

"Sure. Why don't we head over to the hill and take a look? I wouldn't mind seeing it."

"Just the two of us?" the teacher asked, as they slowly moved farther from the crowd.

"Why? Are you scared?"

"In dangerous situations like this, it's important to be prudent, thambi."

"Would you still have objections if we went with a group of people?"

"A group?! I have tried to convince them. I've shouted like a bear, till I went sore in the throat. But not one person is ready to come."

"I've said *I'll* come, haven't I?" Rajendran tried to corner him.

The Tamil teacher hesitated.

By then, Govinda Naicker, his brother-in-law Rajamanickam, and their entourage were leaving. As they walked away, Rajamanickam glanced again in Rajendran's direction.

"Rajamanickam keeps looking at you. He's probably going to be this village's next naataamai, you know."

"There's something about his gaze that seems a little off."

"Something about the man, too. Anyway, let it be, thambi. What shall we do now?"

"What do you mean, what shall we do? Come on, let's go to the hill and have a look!"

The Tamil teacher looked this way and that, but after some more hesitation, he finally began to walk. They ambled down the mud paths of the village, attracting a few curious looks.

"This is a different kind of village. You can count the number of educated people on your fingers. No matter how much you try to teach them, they'll keep doing things the way they're used to. Just my luck, to be stuck in the middle of this bunch as a Tamil teacher," Deenadayalan rambled on as he walked.

"Tell me, how far is the hill?"

"Not too far. You can see it right over there."

Rajendran looked in the direction Deenadayalan was pointing. On one side of the hill, sheer rock walls rose to the height of one or two palmyra trees, with not a bit of vegetation growing on them. Soon the top of the hill came into view; it was covered with thorny bushes and boulders. At the base of the hill was a large meadow and an irrigation canal. The canal was full to the brim.

"We used to play all across this meadow when we were kids—cops and robbers, shooting catapults. Now see how desolate it is."

As the teacher expressed his sadness, Rajendran reached the edge of the meadow. He walked a short distance across the spongy grass and suddenly stood still. There was a slight tremor in the earth below his feet.

CHAPTER 3

RAJENDRAN FELT THE TREMOR run through his body from his feet to the top of his head. Stepping aside quickly, he bent down to look. But there was nothing but ordinary grass.

The teacher was watching his every move. "What, thambi? What are you looking down for?"

"The ground shook. Didn't you feel it?"

"No."

"That's surprising!" said Rajendran as he went back to stand in the same place he had been earlier. This time, he felt nothing.

"What, thambi! You've just now set foot here, and you're already saying the ground is moving! Are you sure it's the earth that's shaking? Or is it your mind?"

It seemed like the teacher was teasing him a little bit. Rajendran felt annoyed. He frowned at him.

"I don't know why, but no matter who comes this way, they all have stories to tell! Cows and goats running away, veshtis catching on fire." The teacher watched as Rajendran looked around carefully.

The scenery was beautiful. A breeze caressed the surface of the water in the canal, causing little waves to form; their crests and troughs looked like lines of poetry. The canal bank was covered with grass spread out in a green carpet, each blade laden with dew. The rocky hill appeared like the head of a giant demonic *asura*, with waves of *pirandai* creepers cascading down the boulders like hair.

On one of the nearer rocks stood a garden lizard, its front two legs outstretched like a runner at the starting blocks. It peered down at Rajendran and the teacher.

"See, thambi, what a picturesque place this is! It's hard to believe there's anything threatening going on here, isn't it?"

Rajendran nodded in agreement. "Okay, come. Let's go up the hill and have a look," he said.

"What?" The Tamil teacher's faltering tone betrayed his feelings. "No… it doesn't seem so wise to me, just the two of us going alone."

"What are we to do, then? On the one hand, you say no one else from the village will come. Then you say that it isn't wise for us to go by ourselves. Meanwhile you keep saying it's unlikely that we have anything to fear! I am just not able to understand you!"

"Thambi, I am very clear. I'm not afraid of spirits or any of that nonsense. But as I wrote in the letter, I think there's an escaped convict out here who's up to some tricks. Ramasamy's already dead, and I don't think we should be in a rush to add ourselves to the tally. If we go there, I'm sure he'll do something to try to scare us."

"So let's just not get scared."

"But what if he attacks us? Say he throws a knife at us from somewhere?"

Rajendran scratched his chin. He had to admit there was some logic in the teacher's question.

"Now you understand what I am saying. I think we need to gather some people and surround the hill on all sides. If we go in as a large group, then we'll be able to catch him without anyone getting hurt."

"Fine, then let's get a group together."

"Yes. But we can't do anything right now. Tomorrow morning the two of us will go to the police station in the next village and file a complaint. There's a big difference between me going alone and me going with an important journalist like you. The police won't ignore what you have to say. We'll come back with ten or fifteen policemen and everything will get sorted out."

Rajendran saw some elegance in this plan. But he wondered where he could spend the night in the village. The teacher continued, answering his unasked question.

"Thambi, what are you worrying about? You can stay in my house. It's just me at home. It's been many years since my wife went to heaven. I have one daughter; she's married to a teacher in Seranmadevi. She comes by to visit me once in a while, and brings my grandson and granddaughter along. I spend the rest of my time reading whatever books I can get my hands on, or just sitting and watching the flowers bloom. Many of us retired village teachers are in the same situation. Thankfully there's a pension to look forward to; aside from that, this profession doesn't have much to offer these days."

The teacher turned around and started walking back towards the village. Rajendran, who had started to hope for some action, felt momentarily cheated. But the wisdom of the teacher's plan restrained him and he quietly followed.

At one spot, he turned back to face the hill with the canal running alongside it. He captured them in his camera. *CLICK!*

* * *

Jhal! Jhal! Over the mud roads of the village came Govinda Naicker's bullock cart. Seated inside was the astrologer, Marthandam Pillai, looking as plump and ruddy as a ripe, red fruit. Sacred ash covered his entire forehead, with a big coin-sized dot of red *kumkum* in the middle. His fingers seemed to be overflowing with gemstone-laden rings and numerous *rudraksha* necklaces hung from his neck.

Suddenly, the bullock cart drew to a halt. Ramasamy's funeral procession was approaching, accompanied by music and dancing; the body was lying on a wooden bier covered in flowers. One man walked a few meters in front of the procession setting off fireworks. The rockets sped across the sky like arrows, leaving trails of fire before bursting in mid-air, sending shock waves through the crowd.

The bullock cart driver pulled the cart to one side. "What man? Is that a dead body coming?" asked the astrologer.

"Yes, sir. It's Ramasamy from our village. The evil spirit struck him down, remember?"

"Oh, that case! Leave it, let them pass. When a man's time comes, Lord Yama will take him, and He will come in whatever form He pleases. This time, the kaathu karuppu seems to have gotten the job done. As far as I am concerned it's a good omen. This indicates that the work I have come for will end well. Things always work out well for Naicker!"

As the astrologer carried on, Ramasamy's body passed by, accompanied by the loud clamour of *thappu* drums. Behind it came the crowd of relations, with Chinna Pechi among them. Some of the women supported her as she walked. A few feet ahead the road curved away, and Pechi and the rest of the women stopped there. The men proceeded onwards to the cremation ground.

The astrologer took in the whole scene from inside the cart. Then the cart driver grabbed the tail of the bullock and manoeuvred the cart back to the centre of the mud road.

As the bullock cart began to move, Pechi seemed to forget herself in her tears. She turned sharply, as if possessed, and glared at the astrologer seated within. Her two bloodshot eyes radiated heat as she stared at him. That stare completely unnerved the astrologer. The bullock cart began to pick up pace.

The biggest brick house in Aayakudi belonged to Govinda Naicker. The front yard was huge: big enough to fit two volleyball courts! To one side, sheaves of harvested paddy were being tied in bundles. At the front of the house was a large iron grill gate. Naicker's car and tractor entered through the gate, and behind them came the bullock cart. The sound of the jangling bells around the bullock's neck announced the arrival of the astrologer.

Govinda Naicker was on the terrace. His barber was shaving his armpits. It was a delicate task; even the slightest jerk could result in bleeding. So, without turning, Naicker asked, "*Tha!* Who's come now?"

Some servants hurried over to him.

"It must be the *josiyar*," Naicker said. "Go and see. Put out a bamboo chair under the bottle gourd creeper and seat him there. Tell him I'll come down in a moment; I'll just bathe first." The servants ran to attend to the guest.

The astrologer, having alighted from the bullock cart, was taken to the front of the house, where the bottle gourd creeper grew lush and green. He was seated in a bamboo chair in the shade of the creeper.

"Aiyya has just gotten his hair cut. He will bathe and then come down. He asked us to let you know."

The astrologer had the habit of chewing betel leaves. Even when he slept, his jaw moved. He kept with him in his shirt pocket at all times a thin silver toothpick with which to pry bits of betel nut from his teeth. It was a sensation in which he took immense pleasure. Anticipating that pleasure, he had just removed the toothpick and was about to start picking at his teeth when he was interrupted.

"Welcome, josiyare," said Rajamanickam, emerging from the house.

"*Vaale*… my young bull!" replied the astrologer.

"So, josiyare, have you fixed a date?"

"That's exactly what I've come to talk to you about."

"Very good! What will you have to eat?"

"The next meal I eat in your house will be the wedding feast!"

Rajamanickam blushed slightly on hearing this. As they spoke, Rajamanickam's elder sister, Vanjiammal—Naicker's wife—came out to see the astrologer, wiping her brow with the long end of her sari.

"*Vaanga!* Welcome, josiyare," she said.

"Where is our young girl?"

"Who? Are you asking about Thenmozhi?"

"Of course."

"She's inside watching TV. Always in front of the TV, my daughter! Then again, if she didn't have that distraction, I don't know how I could ever bear to look at her. Her face is always tinged with sadness."

"Don't worry, after the wedding everything will sort itself out. What brings our *mappillai* Rajamanickam here?"

"This one? What brings him anywhere? Of course, *now* he is all quiet and well-behaved. If only he'd been like that from the beginning, then he and my daughter could have been married a long time ago, and by now there would be at least two grandchildren playing in the house."

"*Akka!* Why are you stirring up old rubbish?" protested Rajamanickam. "I've left my past behind me. I'm a good honest man now, right? See, even today I'm leaving for Tirunelveli to take care of some business for *maama*. Some dog came to him begging and borrowed fifty thousand rupees, and he hasn't even been paying interest! I'm going to go see him and get the money back."

"Then you carry on. I'll speak to the josiyar myself." Vanjiammal sent her brother on his way. Then she turned back to Marthandam Pillai and sighed deeply.

Naicker, freshly bathed, walked out of the house, still drying his wet hair. He greeted the astrologer and sat down.

"In the coming month of *Aavani*, two *muhurthams* match. We can pick either of them, whichever date you prefer," said the astrologer before Naicker could ask.

"*Sandhosham!* Wonderful! You said you were going to recalculate the girl's horoscope. Did you do it?"

"Of course. There is not a single *dosham*; in fact, your daughter's good times are just beginning. For the last seven and a half years, Saturn has tormented her—but those times are in the past."

"So you're saying this wedding will take place without a problem and my daughter's future will be bright?"

"Bring out some camphor and I will swear on it! If I, Marthandam Pillai, say so, it is like Lord Adikesavan himself saying so! It's all in the calculations. Spotless calculations, Naicker!"

"They had better be! There's no shortage of money or prestige, and my girl looks like a princess. But every time we've gone down this path of trying to get her married, I've been humiliated! Not just one or two grooms, either!"

"Aiyya, why bring that up? All of that's behind you now. Your own brother-in-law has been fixed as the mappillai, hasn't he? A wedding is not something *we* determine; it is something that has been planned in the stars long in advance. Everything will happen of its own accord, at the right time."

"*Romba* sandhosham! This time my daughter's wedding must go off without even the smallest hitch. If anything goes wrong, even something minor, both my daughter and I will hang ourselves to death!" said Naicker, his voice suddenly breaking.

"Nothing will go wrong! I promise you that a *thaali* will definitely be tied around your daughter's neck at the auspicious time I have picked," said the astrologer.

As soon as he had spoken, an overripe bottle gourd fell—*bothu!*—on his head, startling him.

To Naicker, it seemed like a bad omen. He looked upset.

They examined the stem of the bottle gourd and found that it was quite firm. They both wondered how it could have fallen like that—all of a sudden, as if it had been cut.

As they looked at the gourd, Chinna Pechi stood outside the grill gate, holding the bars. She watched them intently, a fierceness radiating from her eyes.

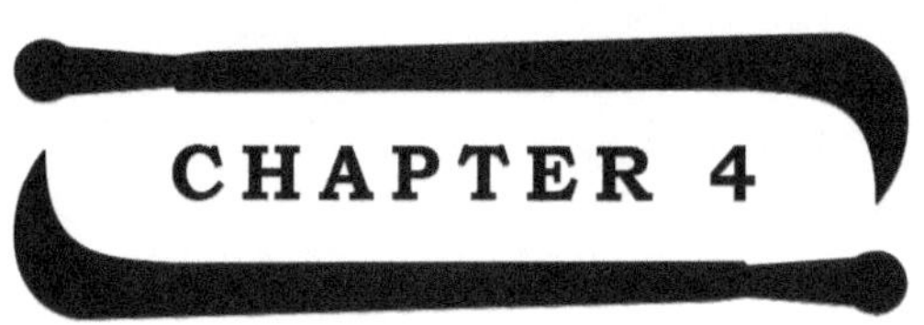

CHAPTER 4

FROM THE OTHER SIDE of the gate, Chinna Pechi's glare seemed to claw at Marthandam Pillai. Govinda Naicker noticed her staring, too.

"Who's that? Looks like our dead Ramasamy's daughter, doesn't it?" he asked, gesturing as he spoke for Chinna Pechi to come in. But she continued to stand where she was, staring at them as if she was about to attack.

"What is with that child? Why is she standing like that?" asked Govinda Naicker.

One of the servants, who was carrying a bundle of grass for the cows, answered him. "Aiyya, she's been like that since her father died. The same spirit that attacked Ramasamy has affected her, too. They say she'll remain like this till the exorcist comes and chases it out of her."

"Fine, but where is the exorcist? Has he crossed the oceans to another country? How can the child be left in this state? Look, just look at the way she is glaring!"

"True sir. But our exorcist has gone on a pilgrimage to Tirupathi."

As they spoke, there was a sudden change in Chinna Pechi. She seemed to come back to normal and walked in calmly through the gate. She wore a dirty *pavadai* with a torn shirt; her hair was matted and her eyes were heavy with grief. She looked like a typical village girl caught in the strong grip of abject poverty, very piteous to look at. Not a drop of her previous stony gaze remained; in fact, now her eyes were beginning to get moist with tears.

Naicker asked in a gentle voice, "Child… what brings you this side? Whom do you want to see?"

"My Appa died."

"Yes, dear, I know. I even came to your house, remember? Don't you worry now, I'm there for you."

"Poor Appa… wrung Appa's neck…" Chinna Pechi was trying to tell Naicker something, but her voice began to crack. "Wrung his neck! Wrung his neck!" she repeated, as though stuck on the phrase. Her breath became laboured, her cheeks swelled up, and her face began to contort into a rage. Her sudden transformation frightened even Naicker.

At that moment one of the servants took hold of her and dragged her away. Naicker turned to the astrologer, his face full of worry. The astrologer was rattled as well.

"Josiyare! Did you see how much that young heart is yearning? She tried to say something about her father's neck being wrung, but she couldn't finish. What if somebody killed Ramasamy by strangling him?"

"It must have been written in his horoscope that he would die the way he did. Anyway, now he is gone. What's the use of investigating it? Let's get back to the business of Thenmozhi's wedding."

"What is there to get back to? Just as you were talking about the auspicious date a bottle gourd fell on your head! That doesn't exactly seem to portend well."

"*Aiyyaiyyo!* Don't worry about that! This time around, the thaali will definitely be tied around your daughter's neck. I have no doubt about it. In ten days Raahu's influence will wane and Jupiter will rule her horoscope. We've been stuck all this time because of Raahu. Jupiter is a good planet for your daughter; it's sitting in a good position as well. Auspicious Mars is also at his zenith. That's why I say there's nothing that can keep your daughter from getting married now. I will swear to it!"

Standing inside the house near the window, Thenmozhi was listening to everything they said.

"Ask your daughter to offer milk at the sacred termite mound where the snakes live, without fail," the astrologer went on. "Also, ask her to tie a grass garland for the Ganesha idol. The snake mound is representative of Raahu; the milk that she offers there will serve to ward off any misfortune that Raahu can bring about. The Ganesha represents Ketu, Raahu's opposite, and the grass offering will strengthen Him, helping to overcome any obstacles."

This advice also fell on the ears of Vanjiammal, who had gone into Thenmozhi's room.

"Hey, girl! You heard, no? You better do everything the josiyar says. This time around your wedding absolutely has to happen!"

"Why, ma? You mean if I don't do all those things, I won't have to get married?" she questioned.

"What are these questions you're asking? We're being given chances here to help bring about good fortune. It's up to us to grab hold of them—*gappu!*" She mimed catching something in her hand. "Like that!"

"Good fortune? To spend the rest of my life with Rajamanickam? I don't…." She trailed off before finishing her sentence.

"*Adiye!* I know very well what you want to say. But given the position we're in now, finding anyone else will be nearly impossible! The news of your oh-so-wonderful horoscope has spread everywhere! The talk is that bad luck will befall any family that even considers a prospective alliance. Don't forget everything that's happened up till now," Vanjiammal scolded her daughter. "Go and offer your prayers to God at the right time. Oh, only I know how troubled my heart is…"

Thenmozhi's face was drained of emotion. She looked out through the window and saw the astrologer leaving.

Naicker sat, scratching his jaw, deep in thought.

* * *

Deenadayalan's house was full of books. All the covers had been wrapped in brown paper with the titles written neatly on the wrappers. It was a small house with a tiled roof, simple but elegant.

There was a single rope cot with a blanket and a pillow, tempting anyone who laid eyes on it to lie down and have a nap. Rajendran was admiring the house. He took a few books from the bookshelf and looked at them. Bharathidasan's *Kudumba Velakku*—"The Family Lamp". Kannadasan's *Arthamulla Hindu Madham*—"Meaningful Hinduism". Saandilyan's *Jala Deepam*—"Waterlight". Na Parthasarathy's *Kurunji Malar*—"Kurunji Blossoms". Kalki's *Alai Osai*—"The Sound of Waves". All books by legendary writers.

"You are very well read," he praised the Tamil teacher, as he flipped through the books. Suddenly, one book made his face change. *Aavigaludan Pesalaam*— "Let's Talk to Spirits" read the cover. The title plucked a smile from between his lips.

"They really print books like this?"

"Why, thambi? You don't believe in all this spirit business?"

"Do you?"

"It's not just me. Everybody's on the fence about this subject."

"Not me, I'm not on the fence. The only spirits I believe in come in bottles!"

The Tamil teacher laughed at this, but didn't reply.

"Why aren't you saying anything?"

"What else to say? I've already told you, I'm of two minds on this issue."

"Hmm... But then how come, when it comes to your own village, you don't believe in ghosts? You even sent us a letter refuting their existence."

"My eyes fell on that convict. Otherwise I doubt if I would have written to your magazine."

"So if you hadn't seen him, you'd believe that hill was haunted? I think this book has gotten to you."

"That I don't know. But there's one thing I am certain of—there is definitely a soul, something that stays within us all our living days. Where does it go when we are no more? That is a question yet to be answered."

"So according to you, the soul leaves the body after death and... goes somewhere?"

"You don't think so? For so many years it resides in the body, controlling everything; only when it leaves does the body become a corpse. When the soul is inside the body, the body reacts to things. If it's pricked by something, even a tiny thorn, it lets out a scream of pain. But when the soul has departed, that same body can be hacked to pieces and it won't do so much as twitch."

"Fair enough. Even rationalists speak of peace for the soul after death. They mark a day of remembrance for the departed—sometimes they even erect statues. But what I don't get is this talk of the soul roaming around as a ghost or a demon. I mean, let's examine that for a minute. Crores of people have died over the years. Shouldn't there be crores of ghosts and spirits around us?"

"Perhaps there's a reason why not all of them become ghosts."

"Okay. So, can we assume that one out of every ten people who dies becomes a ghost?"

"Don't be so simplistic. No one can begin to understand what ghosts are like without having any experience. The ancient texts discuss this subject; maybe they can serve as a good starting point. Of course, if you dismiss those texts as false outright, then even that line of inquiry falls flat."

"Okay, so what does *this* book say?"

"It says we can speak with the dead. It describes many ways to do it."

"Have you ever tried to talk to someone?"

"No... The book says that in order to do that, you need to be able to focus completely on a single point. There should be no other thoughts; apart from the dead person, there should be no one else in your mind. Oh, the book gives plenty of advice like that. But I don't think it's something I'm capable of. Besides, I really haven't felt like talking to any spirits anyway."

"Well, the opportunity hasn't slipped away! Ramasamy died under suspicious circumstances right here in your village. Everyone else believes that his death was due to an evil spirit, but you think that an escaped convict is responsible— and I believe the same too. If a life was taken in this manner, do you think that the soul has found peace?"

"What are you getting at?"

Rajendran came right to the point. "Shall we try talking to Ramasamy, like it says in this book?"

The teacher seemed to consider the idea.

"What do we have to lose?" Rajendran continued. "It isn't like we have any money riding on it. If there is a spirit, maybe it will show up. If there isn't, then it's like I said earlier—they're only found inside bottles of alcohol!"

"Fine, thambi—but will you really be able to focus your mind on a single point? To think of nothing and nobody but the dead Ramasamy?"

"I'll try my best. I suppose if his spirit really is wandering around restlessly, it won't care if I don't perform the ritual perfectly. It'll be itching to bring the guilty to justice!"

"What you say makes sense. Okay, let's try it and see what happens."

"Now you're talking! Experience is the only verifiable truth. If we know the truth right now, then we'll have more clarity when we go to the police tomorrow. We can take our next steps confidently."

"Okay thambi. First go have a bath."

"Oh! Are ghosts particular about hygiene?"

"Yes, both the body and mind should be pure—so says the author of this book. Since the body is the medium, it is important for it to be cleansed as well."

"No problem, then! I'll bathe. Where is the bathroom?"

"Ha! Are you joking? This is a village—we don't have any bathroom-geethroom here! I just draw water from the well at the back and bathe right next to it. Or else I go dip myself in the tank near the Sivan temple."

"Then I'll go take a dip in the tank. I'm feeling a bit grimy."

"Fine. Head down this street, turn left, and keep going straight. You'll end up at the tank. Careful though! It's quite deep and there's a lot of mud at the bottom. Just stay close to the bank and then come back. If anyone asks, tell them you're my relative, and I'll handle it."

"Okay." Moving energetically, Rajendran picked up a towel, changed into a lungi and left.

"By the time you get back, I'll have some rava upma ready," said Deenadayalan, heading towards the kitchen.

The Sivan temple tank was green with algae. Rough granite steps led down to the water on all four sides. A few people stood around washing clothes on the steps. At the centre of the tank was a small structure; inside it sat a group of men playing cards. Rajendran watched them as he walked down the stone steps and stood with his feet in the water. He ventured deeper so that he could get done with his bath before it became dark. There was a chill in the air. He plunged into the water and immersed himself fully, and the chill went away.

He finished his bath and made his way back up the steps. No one stopped him to ask anything.

Beside the tank was a peepal tree, and at its base was a Pillaiyar idol. Thenmozhi was there, putting a grass garland around the idol.

Rajendran, a Pillaiyar devotee himself, turned and began to walk around the tree in prayer.

Just as he started, Thenmozhi, unaware of his presence, began addressing the god. "Pillaiyar Appa!" she said. "Earlier, I used to feel bad every time my wedding preparations ground to a halt. But this time I'm more worried about the plan actually going through. Oh, I don't want this wedding to happen!"

Rajendran heard this, wondering what it was all about. Just as she finished, a voice rang out, seemingly out of nowhere. "It won't happen," said the voice. "This wedding won't happen." Then it fell quiet.

Rajendran stood still, astonished.

CHAPTER 5

THE VOICE SEEMED TO HAVE BEEN carried into Rajendran's ears on the wind. Instantly alert, he stood upright and looked around in all directions. There was no one.

Thenmozhi had finished her prayer. She touched her cheeks, showing respect to the god, and began to walk around the idol. She stopped short when she saw Rajendran. For any girl born and raised in Aayakudi, seeing a new person was always a great surprise. He stared back at her in a sort of daze, still thinking of the mysterious voice and Thenmozhi's unusual prayer to god. Each person was very novel to the other—and so they stood, their gazes colliding.

After a point Thenmozhi could not bear it any more. She turned around and walked away quickly.

She was very good looking—every single feature was perfect. No one with good taste could fail to admire her. And in the young, whenever love comes knocking, the heart is ready to follow it down the path.

A youthful rush of desire came over Rajendran. Just then, someone walked by. Rajendran asked him, "Aiyya, you're from this village, aren't you?"

"Yes, and?"

"See that girl over there, walking away? Who is she?"

"Who do you think you are, man? Asking me about a girl from my own village! That too, our naataamai's daughter!"

"Well, I'll admit she's a very pretty girl. But, that aside, she was praying for her upcoming wedding to be called off. That's what got me wondering."

"What are you blabbering? Finally, after so many obstacles, her marriage has been arranged—her own maama is the bridegroom. The preparations are underway for a grand wedding with plenty of pomp and ceremony! How do you expect anyone to believe she would pray for her own wedding to be cancelled? Who are you, anyway?"

"I'm related to the Tamil teacher, Deenadayalan—on his son-in-law's side."

"Is that so? Fine. But listen, don't tell anyone else what you just told me. If by any chance your news should reach that fellow Rajamanickam's ears, then you're done for!"

"Why should *I* get into trouble? She prayed out loud; I happened to hear it. So, I asked."

"Whatever fell into your ears, let it remain right there. That poor girl has had no luck at all getting married. Now, at last, everything is falling into place. She's probably still scarred by what happened in the past. She's afraid it will happen again; that must be why she's praying the wedding gets called off."

"So she's had a bunch of previous engagements that didn't work out?"

"You're not from around here, that's why you don't know much about it. Go ask that Tamil teacher, he'll tell you lots of stories. Our naataamai has a heart of gold. I don't know what sins he committed or when, but now his bad karma is playing havoc with this poor girl Thenmozhi's life." The man sighed and walked away.

There was a great mystery behind Thenmozhi's story, and Rajendran felt he had to get to the bottom of it.

The scent of the Tamil teacher's upma welcomed Rajendran as he walked in the door. Cooking aromatic food is a great art; it can spark a special kind of joy to catch a whiff of a piping hot meal while one's eyes savour the food at the same time. Rajendran's mouth watered, and he felt an eager hunger through every inch of his body.

He restrained himself, changed his clothes, and sat down next to the Tamil teacher to tell him what he had heard Thenmozhi say at the temple tank. The teacher was astonished.

"Ey, thambi, you sniffed out a story even when you went to bathe. Now I understand why they say that reporters have extraordinary talents!"

"Aiyya, give me an answer. Why did her wedding plans get called off before?"

"What can I say? You can sum it up in one word: fate. That's all it is."

"That's the talk of an illiterate person. You're a teacher! You mustn't talk like that."

"How else should I talk? In our country, as soon as you say the word 'wedding', you're automatically talking about horoscopes, dowries, gifts, and all sorts of other customs and rituals."

"The dowry can't be an issue for a girl like Thenmozhi. She's the daughter of a wealthy zamindar—that too, an only child."

"So it was with Sita. She was King Janaka's only daughter. Even so, she had to go and struggle in the jungle with Rama, and finally she got kidnapped by Ravana! Could King Janaka have done anything to prevent it?"

"Oh, what's the point of these irrelevant examples from the epics? Why has Thenmozhi had so much trouble getting married?"

"Her horoscope is like that. Not just one or two prospective grooms— *many* have come to meet her. They all sound positive, tell the family that they will get back to them—and then, complete silence. One groom even got into an accident soon after meeting with her and lost his life."

"Really?"

"Yes, thambi. Our naataamai, Govinda Naicker, has declared that he would transfer the title of all his lands and wealth to the groom. Despite that, not a single person has come forward to tie a thaali around her neck."

"This is all so astonishing! Why such intense fear?"

"Fear, ah? Let me tell you about the most recent instance… a boy named Ganesan. I knew him. He seemed like a really nice boy, good as gold. Very progressive in his outlook."

"Okay, and what happened to this Ganesan?"

"He saw Thenmozhi at the temple and immediately fell for her. Ganesan's hometown was Aathur, past Thiruchendur—he was actually distantly related to me. He came straight to me and asked about Thenmozhi. I told him all the details."

"'Maama… Maama!' he told me, 'I will marry Thenmozhi! These stars and signs and horoscopes are all a big fraud. I refuse to even give one paisa of respect to any of it. And when I do marry Thenmozhi, it won't be to get hold of all her father's lands and property. I love her from the bottom of my heart. I could never marry anyone other than her. If she put her faith in me and came with nothing but her wedding sari, I would be perfectly satisfied.'

"At first, I thought he was just rambling, driven by a youthful infatuation. But from that day on, the boy was always by the side of the temple tank, like he was carrying out some kind of penance. Every time that girl came by, he stood in front of her and smiled. Eventually she told her father about him. He had Ganesan picked up, and asked him what he thought he was up to.

"Ganesan was unflinching. 'Aiyya, I love your daughter with all my heart. If I do not get her, I will surely hang myself to death.' The naataa-mai was stunned. Then he burst out, 'So you want to marry my daughter. See that snake mound over there? Let's see you put your hand inside it,' he taunted him. He thought he had the boy trapped. But that boy stuck his hand—*posukku!*—right inside the snake mound!"

The Tamil teacher took a break in the middle of his narration to take the upma vessel off the stove. A bundle of plates, made of almond leaves stitched together, lay in one corner of the kitchen. From this bundle he took two and placed them on the bare floor in front of Rajendran. He poured water into a brass lota—*maluk, maluk!*—and then sprinkled some water on the leaves to clean them.

"Aiyya, so then what happened to Ganesan?" asked Rajendran impatiently.

"What do you think happened? Inside the mound was a ten-foot-long black cobra! It bit him. Naicker was shaken, and they immediately took Ganesan to a doctor. I went along too. Somehow, at the last minute, we grabbed hold of that life that was about to slip away and stopped it from leaving his body. Ganesan survived.

"Naicker came around after that, and decided to get Thenmozhi married to him. She was wholeheartedly in agreement. The only problem was that the boy wasn't earning much. So Naicker told him, 'Quit your job. I'll build you a big complex with a grocery store in Tirunelveli.' At first the boy would not accept this offer. It hurt his pride; he thought people would whisper behind his back that he'd only married Thenmozhi for the store. I appreciated his sense of self-respect. But Naicker told him, 'I'm doing all this so that my daughter can live well. Don't worry about what the village says, we'll deal with that later. First let's build the complex and set up the shop.'

"He called the josiyar, Marthandam Pillai, and asked him to pick a good date. The josiyar selected one. Fine, we all thought: Thenmozhi's time of relief has come.

"But then this boy Ganesan heaped sand on all our heads. He stole the ten lakhs that Naicker had kept in his house for the construction of the complex and made his escape!"

The Tamil teacher brought the upma close to his mouth. Then he saw the look on Rajendran's face and stopped.

"What are you thinking, thambi?"

"I can't believe this story!"

"I couldn't believe it either at first. But it's been forty days since he disappeared. Someone came and said they saw him in a club in Bombay, drinking and playing cards. *'Cha!'* was all I could say when I heard that."

"Didn't Naicker file a police complaint?"

"No, his hot-headed brother-in-law did it for him. But still, Ganesan hasn't been caught till date.

"Naicker was broken, unable to bear the betrayal. That's when Raja-manickam came forward and said that *he* would marry Thenmozhi. Now, the wedding's all arranged. But from what you've just told me, it looks like this ceremony might not happen either."

"Why didn't Rajamanickam come forward earlier?"

"He is a rowdy fellow, thambi. He spends more days inside the jail than he does outside. Who will willingly get their daughter married to a guy like that?"

"Oh! Now I understand why that girl prayed to god that way. She doesn't want to marry a thug."

"Naicker doesn't like it either. But if they let this chance slip by, she might remain unmarried her whole life."

The teacher turned the upma over. It had cooled down. "Please eat. Let's stick to our own problems."

"The moment I laid eyes on Thenmozhi, I felt a deep sympathy for her. I can't explain it."

"Don't get involved in this, thambi! Don't you start getting all lovey-dovey! Focus on the task you came here for. We'll solve the mystery of the hill. We have to make sure that convict doesn't get away."

The Tamil teacher began to eat his upma as he spoke. He poured out some puli saaru that he'd made the day before to go with the upma.

Rajendran hadn't eaten all day. The upma tasted divine. As he gobbled it up, his mind was racing, working through multiple calculations.

Finally, he finished his meal, stepped outside, and sat on the comfort-able red-oxide topped *thinnai*.

The Tamil teacher sat in front of him, holding the book *Let's Talk to Spirits*. He also had with him an aluminium tumbler, a small notebook, and a pen.

"What's all this for?"

"Didn't we agree to talk to the spirit? Here, you'll be the medium. Hold the pen and open the notebook. Like I said earlier: empty your mind of all other thoughts. Focus it on a single point. Meditate on the dead Ramasamy. If you can concentrate seriously and deeply enough, his soul will enter your body. Then the spirit will tell us, through your writing, what it is thinking."

"Are you sure about this?"

"This is the first time for me as well. How do I know if it will work? Let's see what happens."

"Okay, I will try whole-heartedly. Even if all this stuff is a lie, I'll do my best to believe in it. It's true that Ramasamy once lived; and it's true that now that life is gone. Let whatever it is that left his body come now to remove our confusion." He sat cross-legged and upright, like an ascetic in meditation.

The teacher swept the area and lit two incense sticks, transforming it into a space worthy of a sacred rite. The smoke from the incense sticks twisted and turned, slithering like a snake through the air before dissipating. Shutting his eyes with conviction, Rajendran tried to focus as he had promised.

Slowly the seconds stretched into minutes—one, two, three, and then on and on.

It was almost completely silent. Somewhere, from someone else's yard, a cow mooed; but then even that sound stopped.

The Tamil teacher watched Rajendran's serious effort. Then, suddenly, Rajendran's body shivered as if a spirit had entered him. His hand began to write.

Vanakkam, Rajendran thambi! I am Ramasamy speaking. And your guess is correct: I was murdered.

And it's not just me. That poor boy Ganesan—they killed him too.

The Tamil teacher read the words as they appeared, and his jaw dropped.

CHAPTER 6

Rajendran, now a spirit medium, kept writing. Deenadayalan continued to watch him with his mouth still open.

Poor Ganesan! He came to the canal to have a bath. Rajamanickam and his men killed him. By chance I happened to witness it, so Rajamanickam strangled me to death. My daughter watched as I was killed. Fortunately, because she was hiding, neither Rajamanickam nor his men noticed her. If they had, my daughter would be a corpse now too. The spirit which keeps possessing my daughter is Ganesan's. It won't stop until it kills Rajamanickam. If it succeeds, my daughter will be seen as a criminal, and I will be devastated. It seems as if God himself has come to my aid through you. For truly, if not for this effort on your part, I would have been unable to act!

Thambi, somehow, please save my daughter. You must show everyone that Rajamanickam is the real criminal. Please try and make contact with me regularly. I can tell you about the true feelings of Ganesan's soul, and also about Rajamanickam's schemes. On the sixth day of the lunar month, the same day that I breathed my last, please have my daughter pay her respects by the riverside.

Crores upon crores of thanks to you.

With that, the pen that Rajendran was writing with stopped moving. His body shuddered again; he shook himself off like a wet crow, and in that moment, he returned to being the same Rajendran as before. He read what he had written in his trance. Wonder and shock made his eyebrows arch upwards. The Tamil teacher stared at him, dumbfounded.

"What is this, Aiyya?" Rajendran asked. "Did I write this?"

"Why, thambi? Are you doubtful?"

"This is not my handwriting!"

"Then it must be Ramasamy's writing. Wasn't it his spirit that entered your body?"

"Does that mean my very first attempt was a success?"

"It certainly seems so."

"Incredible! Do you think anyone else will believe us if we tell them?"

"Who cares what anyone else believes! Look at what Ramasamy has said. This is a terrible tragedy!"

"Yes, it's tragic... if it's true."

"You're still not convinced?"

"I mean, can this really be real? I have so many questions now!"

"What sort of questions?"

"Ramasamy's spirit entered me and told us all these things. Why couldn't he have entered Naicker's body, and told him instead?"

"How would that be possible? *You* made an attempt to contact the spirit, so he came. Naicker would have had to try to contact him too, no?"

"No... Somehow it doesn't quite make sense to me that he would only come when summoned. The ghost needs to manifest himself in order to reveal the truth about what happened. Only then will the agony of his death have some kind of meaning. If he says he'll only talk if someone calls him... That doesn't seem right."

"But hasn't the other ghost been possessing that girl Pechi in exactly the way you said, without her calling him? That look in her eyes, her nervous energy... doesn't it all seem frightening to you?"

"That's true, isn't it."

"If she does something to Rajamanickam in that angry state, society will brand her as a murderer—just as Ramasamy said in the note! Do you think any court will accept the defence that she was possessed by a spirit when she killed him?"

"So you think that's why Ramasamy didn't just enter someone's body unbidden?"

"That seems like the logical conclusion, if we go by the letter."

"So you believe it all? Everything Ramasamy has said in this letter?"

"You still have doubts, after all this discussion?!"

"Yes! I can't *not* doubt that this is real. Births and deaths are happening all the time—if this is really how things worked, wouldn't there be a medium to communicate with the dead in every house?"

Rajendran's question made the teacher smile a little.

"What's wrong with what I asked? Why are you smiling?"

"I smiled not because of your question, but at the mind that thought of the question. You find it so hard to believe in anything. Scepticism comes so easily to you."

"Come back to the point. On what basis do we believe this letter?"

"Thambi, I wouldn't put it past Rajamanickam to murder someone. I think the chances are good that things happened exactly the way Ramasamy has described them."

"Okay. If we go show this letter to Naicker, do you think he'll accept that it's true? Won't he assume it's just another way to halt his daughter's wedding?"

"You might be right there, thambi. But, let me ask you one thing. You wrote this letter yourself, without being aware that you were doing it. Isn't that right?"

"Yes."

"Then let's leave everybody else out of it for a moment. How can *you* still doubt that it's true?"

"For the same reason I gave you earlier. If the dead could freely speak their minds, wouldn't every family be speaking to their dead relatives every single day? Actually, why bring anyone else's family into it—why can't *I* converse with *my* dead grandparents?"

"Thambi, you're asking all the right questions. That's why Ramasamy said to stay in contact, and that he would do what he could."

"But what does that mean?"

"Why don't you ask Ramasamy himself what it means? Let's see what he says."

"But isn't it madness to ask the very source you doubt to clarify your doubts?"

"Fine… then we can try another way."

"What's that?"

"Ramasamy told us that Ganesan's spirit was inside Pechi. Let's test to see if that's true."

"That's an idea. But leave that aside for a minute; when are we going to the hill to look for that convict?"

"Ah! You're right, all this talk of spirits has pushed that to a corner."

"And if you ask me, that's the most important matter at hand. An escaped convict in hiding, deceiving the cops—it's nothing short of treason! Knowing about it and not doing anything is irresponsible."

"What you say is correct. But look, it's dark now. There's no point in going to the police at this hour. We can only go tomorrow."

"Then shall we go see that girl?"

"Yes, thambi. Let's get going." The teacher rose, picked up the towel that was hanging on the edge of the wooden door, and put it across his shoulder. Rajendran stood in front of an old, spotty mirror, bending and twisting to see himself clearly. He combed his hair and then left with the teacher.

On the outer wall of the house was a shelf, and on the shelf was a tin box filled with *vibuthi*. On their way out, the teacher grabbed a fistful of the sacred ash and smeared lines of it across his forehead. He dropped a small pinch into his mouth as well. Then he took another fistful and turned to Rajendran. "One minute," he said, and pulled his fingers across Rajendran's forehead.

"What? Why put all this ash on your forehead now?"

"This vibuthi is from the Ayyanaar temple, the guardian deity of our village. It will protect you from the evil spirits."

"Oh… so it's a precaution?"

"We're going to meet a girl who has been possessed by a spirit, after all. What if the ghost decides to enter our bodies while we're with her? I'm not keen on having an exorcist beat it out of me with bundles of neem leaves!"

"You're completely convinced that Ganesan's spirit is inside Pechi?"

"Even if I'm a teacher by training, I'm still a villager at heart. We tend to take things at face value. For that matter, didn't you tell me you heard a disembodied voice say 'It won't happen, this wedding won't happen'?"

"Oh, why do you have to bring that up? Even thinking about it gives me goose bumps."

"It could have been the dead Ganesan's voice. Whatever it is, we'll find out more if we go now and talk to the girl," said Deenadayalan, as he started walking.

Rajendran thought there was some sense in this.

Just then, his editor called him on his cell phone. Rajendran spoke to him as he walked through the streets of Aayakudi.

"Hello sir. Tell me."

"What should I tell you? You're the one who has to report. Where have your efforts got you?"

"For now, I am staying at the Tamil teacher's house. Tomorrow morning, we're going to the police. With their team, we're planning to take care of the escaped convict issue."

"We won't have any interesting news till tomorrow, then?"

"I'd say we already have some. But you aren't going to believe it!"

"What is it?"

"I just spoke with Ramasamy's ghost."

As soon as he heard this, the editor started laughing on the other end.

"I knew it, sir. I knew you'd laugh. But it doesn't matter—-in a way I'm glad you did."

"What are you saying?"

"What's more important than speaking to the ghost is figuring out how much of what he said to believe. We're on our way to test something that the ghost told us."

"Rajendran... you're a sensible journalist. Proceed as you see fit. Just don't slip up and do anything foolish. That is all I'm going to say."

"Definitely sir. I'll be mindful of that. At the same time... it's going to be difficult to get you to believe me when I tell you what I've just experienced."

"Why do you say that?"

"Because there's no way for me to prove it to you; the only way you'll ever believe it is if you take my word for it. Today I heard a voice from nowhere saying, 'This wedding will not happen. It won't happen.' I heard it with my own ears and that's the solemn truth. But I can't make you hear it and prove it you."

"Listen... just focus on what lies ahead. Good or bad, your experiences are important to our readers. One approach is to report nothing but the facts. Another approach is to say things that are totally unbelievable, and stir up a debate. You know our newspaper usually takes the second route. So go ahead courageously. Experience both sides of the issue first-hand and write about that. This will be a novel story for our audience to hear."

After this pep talk, the editor ended the call.

Deenadayalan had been listening as he walked. "Was that your editor?"

"Yes, aiyya. I told him I that spoke with a spirit. Immediately he laughed."

"I figured as much from your responses."

"Does it bother you, the way he's mocking the whole idea of talking to spirits?"

"No, it doesn't bother me… See, everyone else in the village is minding their own business. We are the only ones sticking our noses into something that doesn't need to concern us. And on top of it, we're grappling with the question: to believe or not to believe?"

"That's true too," Rajendran agreed as he walked.

Up ahead, Ramasamy's house came into sight. They could see the heads of a few people sitting outside. As Deenadayalan and Rajendran approached, they turned to look.

"Come, *vaadhyar*, please sit."

"That's all right, I'm fine standing. Have Ramasamy's last rites been completed at the cremation ground?"

"By now his body must have burned down to ashes. We'll go tomorrow morning to sprinkle milk and finish the rituals."

"Okay. Where is that girl Chinna Pechi?'

"Oh, don't ask about her! She's just roaming around wherever she pleases. The exorcist has gone on a pilgrimage to Tirupathi, it seems. Of all the times to be away! We don't know what to do with her."

"Where's the child now?"

"You'll have to go look for her. She won't stay in one place!"

Hearing this, Deenadayalan and Rajendran turned around and began looking for Chinna Pechi.

"Where could she have gone?"

"Come, let's go search. This place isn't like your big city. It's just a tiny village—four or five lanes, one temple, the temple tank, the canal, and the meadow near the hill. That's all."

Their legs walked energetically through the village, searching. It was very dark. The panchayat had installed a few street lights here and there, and those spots alone shone bright in their eyes. The village kids were busy playing hopscotch under the lights. Chinna Pechi was not among them.

They searched everywhere around the houses. Finally, they came to the temple tank. The entire area seemed to be frozen in darkness. There was no sound except for the wind whispering in the trees. From the gopuram of the temple, a light from a small bulb shone. That was all.

"So, teacher, we've looked through the whole village but we haven't seen the girl. What if she went to the canal?"

"Yes, that's the only place we haven't been yet. But… going there at this time of the night?"

"We started something, now let's see it through. We can't let fear hold us back!"

"Fine, let's go and see what happens. We'll carry a stick along as a precaution," said the teacher, breaking a branch from the nearest tree and fashioning a walking stick from it.

He walked along, leaning on the stick.

To get to the canal, they had to go via the main road. Just as they reached the road, they heard a sound. *Thadda! Thadda!* Rajamanickam was approaching on his motorbike. As he passed, he looked hard at Rajendran and the Tamil teacher.

"Thambi, our villain is watching us."

"Let him. You look for that girl."

"Come on, it's just a bit further," said the teacher, as he began taking longer strides.

They came to the canal. As they got closer to the bank, they saw a doll-like figure sitting under a tree. As it stood up, they realised it was Pechi.

"Who is it? Why are you here?" asked the girl in a voice that was unmistakably a man's.

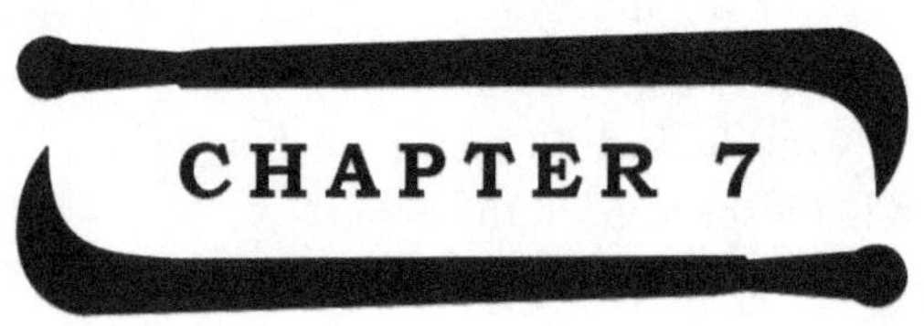

CHAPTER 7

CHINNA PECHI'S STRANGE VOICE and demeanour stunned Rajendran and the teacher. They looked worriedly at each other. The darkness was intense; and yet a fierce light seemed to glow in Chinna Pechi's eyes.

"Ey! I'm asking you a question! What work do you have here at this time of the night?" asked Chinna Pechi, threateningly.

"What is this, Pechi? Why are you changing your voice and scaring us like this? Your mother's been looking for you everywhere. And here you are!" Somehow, the teacher managed to keep his voice steady in front of her. Rajendran shot him a look of amazement.

"No, vaadhyar! Don't tell me lies about them looking for me. Please, go away. There will be a murder here tonight. If you stay here, they'll kill you too!"

"Murder!" Deenadayalan said, stunned. "What are you saying, *aatha*?"

"I am not aatha, vaadhyar!"

"Th-then?"

"Don't you recognize my voice?"

"I'm… I'm not sure…" the teacher said, hesitating.

"I'm Ganesan. Ganesan from Aathur."

"Ganesan! The same Ganesan that left the village and ran off to Mumbai?"

"I didn't leave just the village, vaadhyar, I left the world itself! Yes, I am Ganesan! Dead but still roaming, without any peace... Until I kill Rajamanickam and drink his blood, my spirit will never rest!"

Rajendran felt as though he was being flipped upside-down with each word that Pechi spoke, like a roti over a flame.

"Aiyya! A minute ago, he said a murder was going to take place here. Ask him about that," Rajendran whispered to the teacher.

Without waiting for the teacher to repeat the question, Pechi turned to Rajendran. "Yes, a murder! That convict is hiding here, but he is doomed to die! He was a witness to my murder. Not only that—he is one among those who helped bury me."

"Why have you chosen to possess Pechi?" Rajendran asked. "Couldn't you find anyone else?"

"I do not know," came the answer. "Her body was the only one my soul could enter. My spirit can't get close to anyone else. I can't stay in Pechi's body all the time, either. Even now, I'm about to leave her; I'm not able to hold on. Only when Saturn is ascendant am I able to enter her body. At other times, I can't get in."

As he spoke, Pechi collapsed on to ground. A moment later, she straightened herself, then seemed to take in the situation and the darkness. Frightened, she began to cry. To her, Rajendran and the teacher, standing nearby, appeared as nothing but two dark figures.

"Aiyya! Who are you? Leave me alone. I want to go to my mother. Leave me alone." She flailed her hands about and began crying louder.

The teacher understood at once what had happened.

"Thambi, did you see that? It's beyond anything we imagined!"

"You're right. I don't quite know what to make of it."

"We'll discuss that later. Right now, let's get this child home before it gets too late. Come on."

"But aiyya! You just heard the girl say there's going to be a murder!"

"Yes! Ganesan said that they were planning to kill the convict, no?"

"Aiyya, do you really believe it was Ganesan's soul speaking just now?"

"I heard his voice with my own ears. How can I disbelieve it, thambi?"

"So what Ramasamy said when he was inside me has come true?"

"Yes, that's what must have happened. But come. Let's talk it over after we've dropped this child at home."

"Do we really have to leave this place right now?"

"We can't stay here with the girl. We shouldn't. Let's go."

"No, aiyya, I'm going to stay. You can go drop her and come back."

"*Aiyyo!* No! I won't leave you here alone either. Please just come along."

"Don't be afraid, aiyya. Everything the first spirit said has come true. Now I want to see if what Ganesan's ghost just told us turns out to be true as well. We can't let another murder happen here, that's for certain!"

"Thambi, listen to what I tell you. Staying here by yourself is not a smart idea. Come, we'll go quickly and come back. We need to work together and support one another to get through this."

The teacher pulled him by the hand. Grudgingly, Rajendran started to walk behind them towards the village. In the darkness of the canal bank, they looked like thick black lines on the move.

After they had walked some distance, a thorn pierced Rajendran's sandal. He stopped to pick it out and throw it away. In that instant he felt a vibration.

"Come on, thambi, why did you stop?"

"Aiyya! Just come and stand here."

The teacher went and stood next to Rajendran. Chinna Pechi stared at them vacantly. The teacher, too, clearly felt the tremors.

"Yes, thambi! They say if the earth shakes it will destroy the world. But only this particular place is shaking. There must be something underneath."

As the teacher spoke, Rajendran took out his pen and planted it straight in the ground.

"What are you doing?"

"I've planted the pen as a marker. We'll come here in the daytime and see what's what. Let's go now."

His walking picked up speed. The moon hung in the sky like a slice of watermelon. It was only a few days until ammavasai, the day of the new moon.

* * *

Thenmozhi sat wearily. Vanjiammal came in with a bowl of mashed henna paste and sat next to her. A fat, round light bulb gave out a dim yellow glow to the room.

"Show your hand child! I'll put some henna on for you."

Vanjiammal's gesture was meant as a loving one, to improve her mood. But Thenmozhi was only irritated by it.

"What sort of face is this, *di*? You're a bride, it won't be nice if your hands look plain. Stretch your palm out."

"Oh, go away ma! Marriage, it seems! *Mannankatti!* Useless!"

"Marriage is not useless, di. Right now, *you're* the one acting useless. Stretch your hand out."

"Amma, I don't want to get married. Leave me alone."

"Look here! If your father comes to know how you're behaving, that's all…!"

"I'm the one who's going to have to live with that guy. Not Appa."

"Thenu, don't talk too much! It's true, Rajamanickam wasn't always a good boy. But now that he's going to marry you, he's changed a lot, di. Even we can see that, no? The saying goes that one simple girl can achieve with patience what a thousand geniuses cannot. You will make him an even better person."

"No, ma. I'm not some social worker; it's not my job to reform anyone. I'm just an ordinary girl."

"Look here, if you do anything to put this wedding at risk, neither you nor me will ever see your father in good health again!"

"You've used that same threat to talk me into agreeing to so many things!"

"Well, add this to the list."

Vanjiammal leaned forward and grabbed her right hand and started applying henna to it. The coolness of the henna enveloped Thenmozhi's fingertips, as if there was an ice factory operating under her nails.

The clock's pendulum struck eleven.

* * *

Rajendran and the teacher dropped Chinna Pechi at her home. As they turned to leave, they were surprised by Inspector Rudra, riding towards them on his motorcycle. The beam from his headlight made Rajendran squint his eyes.

Rudra brought his bike to a halt. When he saw the teacher with Rajendran, he said "Vanakkam, sir," respectfully.

"Who's there?"

"It's me, your old student Rudrapathy."

"Oh, Rudrapathy! You're a policeman now?"

"Yes sir, can't you tell by the uniform?"

"Sure. What brings you this far out?"

"That…. well." Rudrapathy seemed like he was about to answer, but then abruptly changed tack.

"I just happened to come this side, to Aayakudi. Listen, has any journalist come to your village?"

"Why are you asking, sir?" asked Rajendran.

Rudra turned to Rajendran, regarding him for a moment. "I need to find this person. Talk to him a little."

"Talk to him a little about what?"

"About something, okay? It's personal."

"Fine, but how did you come to know that he's here?"

"Who are you to question me, thambi?"

"I'm the journalist."

"Oh! Very glad to meet you, Mr. Rajendran. Your editor phoned me up and told me about your assignment. Is there any problem here in the village?"

Rajendran leapt up to shake his hand.

"Sir! God himself must have sent you! The two of us were planning to come and meet you tomorrow. But here you are! I'm very happy. Come, let's go!"

"Where to, Rajendran?"

"To prevent a murder."

"What?!"

"Just come with us. We'll explain later."

The three of them headed speedily towards the hill, walking as if they were in a competition. As they walked, Rajendran told him about the teacher's letter to the newspaper. When he got to the part about the escaped prisoner, Rudra turned angrily to the teacher.

"What, sir? You should have come to me first. Why would you go to a newspaper man?"

The teacher squirmed.

"If even an educated person like yourself hesitates to approach the police, that's not good. If you'd come sooner, I would have caught that convict already. Now we're in a tense situation. How do we know he's even still alive? What if he's been killed?"

"Sir, show your anger later. In fact, we shouldn't even be walking right now. Run, sir!" said Rajendran.

They were approaching the hill. The three of them ran through the dark night. They reached the canal and kept on running along its bank. Suddenly, they came to an abrupt halt. In front of them was a large boulder, and on it lay the body of a man. A burning wooden torch was planted next to it, casting an eerie glow over the corpse.

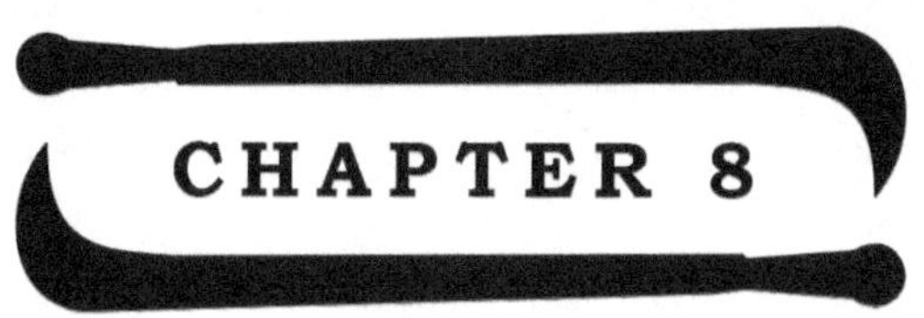

CHAPTER 8

NIGHT CREPT ON, slowly moving towards dawn.

As he stared at the body on the boulder, Rudra felt like a huge nail was being driven into the middle of his head. With a torch in his hand, he went to take a closer look at the body. Then he grimaced and took a couple of steps back.

"Sir! This is the body of the escaped convict. His name is Irumbaadi. In the Palayamkottai prison they called him 'Gangaroo'. He holds the record for the maximum number of escape attempts."

"Looks like he escaped the police only to come and die here, sir."

"True. We need to find out who killed him."

"Who else can it be, sir? It's just as Ganesan's ghost predicted; it is surely the work of Rajamanickam."

"Whatever... let's not talk about it now. Let's get out of here first. I'll inform the station and ask them to make preparations to take the body away. After that we'll talk."

In the darkness, Rudrapathy pulled out his phone and began making calls. The three of them turned to go back.

Rajendran was buried deep in worry. "Teacher, if you had only met Rudra and given a complaint instead of writing to the newspaper, we could have caught this convict alive. Now everything has changed." He clicked his tongue—*tk!*—like a gecko clearing its throat.

"Thambi, how was I to know what would happen? If I'd known earlier that my own student Rudrapathy was the station inspector, I would have gone to the police right away." The teacher seemed to be drowning in a sea of weariness.

Walking through the darkness, Inspector Rudra turned his torch in all four directions, searching.

"I came here thinking this was a minor issue, but it's grown into something very big. One murder for certain, two more deaths that might be murders as well—three in all. And the count could keep increasing."

As Rudrapathy said this, the three of them reached the canal. The stars in the sky shone on the surface of the water as if someone had sprinkled silver powder over the canal. A gentle breeze blew, as though from a hand-held fan, caressing their skin. The surroundings seemed to establish a poetic mood of intense silence.

Here the hillside rose up from the banks of the canal in rough steps. Higher up the slope, they could make out a shape standing on a rock. It appeared to be standing still, statue-like, but the fluttering of a sari edge indicated that it was a woman.

All three of them came to a halt.

"Sir, can you see that up there?"

"I can. It's a woman."

"Are you sure?"

"Can't you see her sari fluttering?"

"She's got some guts, sir! She can see us watching her, and she's still standing there, boldly looking right back at us!"

There was anger in Rajendran's voice. Rudra tried shining the light of his torch towards the rock, but the beam didn't reach far enough. At once, he began to run towards her, hoping to get a better look at her up close, and to catch her.

"Sir!" Rajendran called out to him loudly.

"You stay here. I'll go see who it is." Rudra replied, putting on a good show of speed. His urgency frightened the teacher.

"Rudrapathy! Don't! Come back! We'll go and see in the morning."

Ignoring him, Rudrapathy kept climbing, leaping from stone to stone with the agility of a mountain goat. But the woman who had been standing on top of the rock had disappeared.

"Rajendran, look! She's gone!" The teacher rubbed his eyes.

"You're right. I wonder what's going to happen now," said Rajendran, weary with tension.

Just then they heard the sound of laughter—the voice of a young woman.

"Who's that? Who just laughed?" asked the teacher, nervously.

A raft appeared on the water of the canal. At the edge of the raft was a girl. She sat completely still as the raft began to move fast towards the centre of the canal.

"Thambi! What's going on here?" the teacher's voice rang out.

Rajendran, too, was reeling. He felt there was some sort of magic all around him.

"Come, thambi, let's go. It's a mistake to stay here," said the teacher. Hitching up his veshti, he began to run in the direction of the village.

Rajendran looked up at the hill and then back towards the teacher.

"You go ahead sir," he called out. "Whatever happens, I'll come back with the Inspector."

The teacher ran on until he was lost from sight. Rajendran, now alone, craned his neck to stare up at the top of the hill. The silence began to get to him. He was too embarrassed to show his fear, but too scared to be bold.

He wanted to call out—*Rudrapathy sir! Where are you?*—but he restrained himself.

Just then he heard the sounds of someone approaching from the banks of the canal. He turned back to face that direction. There was a form, misshapen and squashed in the darkness. In one hand it held a stick. In the other, it held something else.

"Aiyya!" it said in a low voice, approaching him closely.

"Who are you?"

"I am just a beggar."

"A beggar?"

"Yes aiyya. Please show some charity."

The form came right up to Rajendran and held out a plate close to his face. *A beggar!? In this dark and deserted place?*

Rajendran's head began to spin. The beggar stepped closer, and Rajendran got a better look at his plate. His insides churned.

There was a severed hand on the plate.

Ey! What is this! Who are you?! A flood of questions rose up within him, but did not cross his lips.

The beggar spoke again, in his pitiful voice. "Aiyya, please give me something, aiyya." Then he walked on past.

Rajendran stood still, rooted to the spot like a tree. Gradually the voice of the beggar faded, and he, too, was lost in the darkness. Rajendran was finally starting to wonder if it had been a mistake not to leave with the teacher.

I shouldn't stay here, he thought; *I'd be safer at the top of the hill.*

He walked up towards it, looking for Rudrapathy. He began his ascent from the base up the slope. As he clambered up the rocks, he paused to have a look around. He heard the sound of someone crying and it made his heart clench. He climbed over another boulder to find a small level stretch of rock on the other side; lying on top of it was another body. Beside its head, a small clay lamp was burning, and by its feet sat a woman with long loose hair, sobbing inconsolably.

He decided to retrace his steps and find another way around. But just as he lifted his foot, it dislodged a small round stone that tumbled down the slope. The sound of the rolling rock broke the silence, ringing out clearly through the night. Rajendran's stomach felt like it was full of acid.

Unable to control himself any longer, he summoned up some courage and called out loudly, "Rudrapathy sir!"

The loudness of his voice echoed all over the rocks. Rudra answered back "I'm here!" His voice, too, bounced off the slopes for a time, and then stopped. Rajendran stumbled in the direction from which the voice came.

Suddenly a beam of light fell on him. It was Rudrapathy's torch.

"Sir!"

"Come on! Here, Rajendran."

"Coming, sir." Rajendran used the light from the torch to pick his way through the rocks to the Inspector.

"Where's the teacher?"

"He ran off. I was waiting for you alone, but I couldn't stay there. In the darkness, there was this beggar…"

"I don't know who the girl I saw was… or *what*… but she was begging, too. Scratching her head furiously while she held out her other hand in front of me. Each of her fingernails was four or five inches long. I saw her face by the light of the torch! Aiyyo! It was horrifying!"

"Sir, I don't think we should keep struggling in the dark here by ourselves. Come on, let's leave and come back in the morning with the rest of your department."

"I'm of the same mind. The darkness and the terrain are our enemy's strength. Are these supernatural visions? Or could someone be orchestrating everything? They say this hill is the domain of evil spirits. Only time will tell which category our experiences fall under. Anyway… let's move."

The two of them began to climb down the hill. Rudrapathy's torch showed the way. They came down the path to where the convict's corpse had been lying. But now, there was no body. The rock was bare.

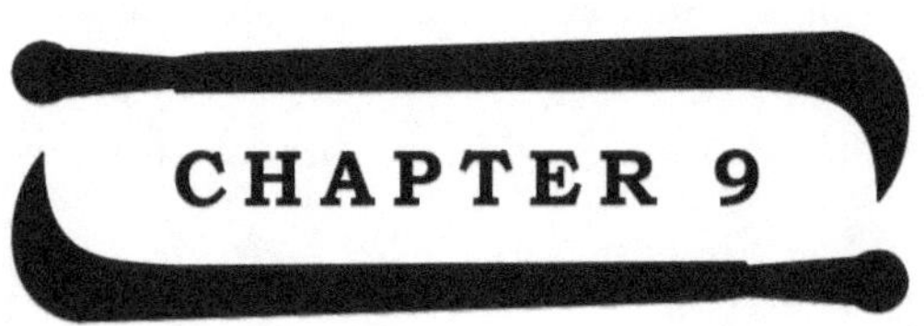

CHAPTER 9

RUDRAPATHY FELT HIS HEAD GO into a spin. At the same time, the sky started to bloom from its greyness. They heard an alarm; the birds woke up and opened their beaks to chirp. Dawn was approaching.

There was only one thing that Rudra was sure of. Some sort of drama had just been staged in front of them. Someone had to be behind it all!

* * *

The teacher's house.

Rudra sat on the rope cot. His forehead itched, full of thoughts. In front of him, lying on the cement thinnai, was Rajendran. His mind was itching just as badly as Rudra's. Deenadayalan was preparing coffee with dried ginger. He poured the fragrant-smelling liquid into two lotas and held them out to Rudra and Rajendran.

"Sir! Is sukku coffee important now? Please sit down. I have lots of questions to ask you," Rudra began, with bluster.

"Rudrapathy, I know what you're going to ask me. I'm ready to answer, too. Even now, if I think about everything that happened last night, neither my hands nor my legs will function!"

"Someone is playing a good game of hide and seek. Can't you see that?"

"I can't accept that explanation."

"You, an educated person?"

"Oh, you say that every time I open my mouth. Rajendran, what's your take?". The teacher tried to stir Rajendran up.

"I'm confused, sir."

"What, do you think we're any better off? We're just as confused as you are!"

"Reporter thambi, what's your opinion of last night's events?" asked Inspector Rudra. He too, wanted to hear Rajendran's views on the matter.

"I'm not able to gauge it, sir."

"You think it's the work of an evil spirit?"

"My better judgement tells me no—but my senses and experiences tell me something else."

"You're all muddled up. Judgements, senses... I don't understand what you're talking about."

"Sir, when I first set foot in this village, I thought all this talk of spirits was just superstition and make-believe. But what the teacher and I experienced right here in this very house made me rethink everything. And when you add last night's events to the mix... I just can't make up my mind."

"Come on. Give me a final answer."

"Sir, something bad has happened here. And it's still happening. I can't completely dismiss the possibility that supernatural forces are involved. That's my final answer."

"What do you mean by 'something bad'? Who's responsible?"

"'Bad' is a simple way of describing it. 'Murder' would be a better word. Not just one murder, but two. If we include the convict we saw last night, that makes it three. And the one responsible is the village naataa-mai's son-in-law, Rajamanickam."

"How are you so sure it's him?"

"Yesterday, we spoke to Ramasamy's ghost. He was the one who told us it was Rajamanickam."

"Look, Mr. Rajendran, you're a journalist. Do you really think educated people are going to believe all this 'I spoke to a spirit' business? In particular, is anyone going to accept a statement like 'The spirit said so, that's why I'm arresting you'? Do you think any of this will stand up in court?"

"Sir, trust me, I understand exactly where you're coming from. Even I was sceptical when we decided to act on what the spirit told us. But everything since then has happened exactly as foretold! How can I help but believe it?"

"And what happened, exactly?"

"Ganesan's ghost told us that the convict would be killed. Didn't that happen just as predicted?"

"Did the ghost give you any other news?"

"Why so many questions, Rudrapathy?" Deenadayalan broke in. "Why are you tearing your head over it? Come on, why don't you speak to Ramasamy's ghost yourself and see?"

"What are you saying, sir?"

"This fellow gave it a try yesterday," the teacher said, gesturing to Rajendran. "You could try it too. Ramasamy told us that he would come and help us whenever we called him. Didn't he?"

"Is that so?"

"He's given it in writing." Deenadayalan got up and showed Rudrapathy the notebook Rajendran had written in when he turned into a medium.

Rudra opened the book. A look of amazement sparked across his face. He finished reading it, and began to pace up and down the room.

"Hey Rudrapathy, why this stomping about?" asked the teacher. "Why don't you try once? Talk to the ghost, like Rajendran thambi did."

"No, sir. If the department came to know about it, I'd be the laughing stock!"

"That's only if they come to know."

"No. First I'll do it my way, then we'll see."

"Your way… meaning?"

"The police way."

In the next instant, he put his cell phone to his ear. He walked a short distance away and began speaking softly to someone.

Rajendran watched him carefully.

"What is it, Rajendran?" Rudrapathy asked after he cut the call.

"Can I join you, as you do it your way?"

"Sure. You're a newspaper man, after all. Come on! Let's go." The two of them left swiftly.

* * *

Water gushed into the fields, pouring out of a large pipe from Naicker's well. The farm workers' children jumped and played in the flow. Thenmozhi walked along the elevated ridge between the fields. The towel on her shoulder indicated that she was headed towards the pump set to bathe. But there was no enthusiasm in her steps.

The fields on either side of her were lush with fully-grown corn stalks. Then… *Vizukk!* Out of the corn, a figure leapt in front of Thenmozhi, startling her. He had a cloth loosely wrapped around his head and face. Only when he unwound the cloth did she realise that it was Rajamanickam.

"What, *pulla*, did I scare you?" Rajamanickam said, grinning.

She glared at him, seething with irritation.

"What's wrong? Why are you scowling at me?"

"What do you want me to do? Do you think this is any way to act, suddenly jumping in front of a girl out of nowhere?"

"I was just playing with you, Thenu. Don't take it the wrong way. Come, let's go sit down and talk for a while."

"No, I'm not coming. Leave me alone."

"What, pulla! Have you forgotten that I'm the one who's going to marry you?"

"We'll see if something like that happens."

"Why do you say that, pulla? You still believe this wedding will get called off, like the other ones?"

Thenmozhi didn't respond.

"What is this, Thenu? Here I am talking to you with so much affection, but you're not uttering a single word. Look, see what I brought for you all the way from Tirunelveli."

Rajamanickam pulled a diamond necklace from the folds of his veshti. It sparkled in the light of the morning sun. Thenmozhi stared at it, dazzled by its brightness.

"So, what do you think? Do you have any idea how much this is worth?"

Thenmozhi remained silent.

"Nearly three and a half lakhs!"

"Really?"

"Yes, *really*. For you, I'm ready to spend even three and a half crores!"

As he spoke, he fastened the necklace around her neck, before she had a chance to stop him.

"Where did you get so much money?" she asked softly.

"Don't you worry about that."

"No, tell me."

"What, do you think I stole it?"

"You've stolen things in the past, haven't you?"

"But this isn't stolen. Trust me."

"Why should I?"

"Okay, I'll tell you the truth. You know that my father left me a piece of land when he died, don't you?"

"Yes. But I thought it was just a barren field, of no value."

"It's true that it's barren. But now a factory is going to come up there. Actually, the fact that it's so rocky is what attracted the builders. They asked me if I wanted to sell the land. What was initially not even worth ten thousand rupees ended up being sold for three and a half lakhs!"

Thenmozhi stood there, still unsure whether to believe Rajamanickam or not.

Meanwhile, Rajendran and Rudra were walking up through the field to meet with Rajamanickam.

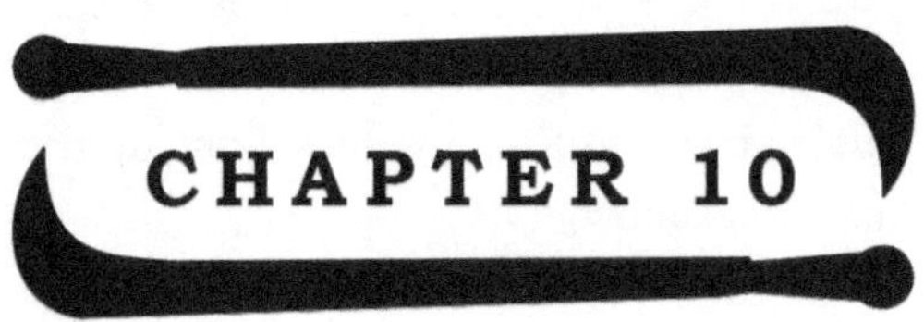

CHAPTER 10

RAJAMANICKAM NOTICED THE TWO MEN approaching. Thenmozhi blinked nervously.

Rudra walked up to them.

"Welcome, Inspector. What brings you so far?" There wasn't a drop of fear or panic in the way Rajamanickam greeted them.

"Just here to see you, Rajamanickam." Rudra, too, took a familiar tone, as if he was speaking to an old acquaintance.

"If you wanted to meet me, why didn't you just come home? Why come out here to the fields?"

"Oh, have they passed some law against meeting people in fields that I don't know about? Rajendran, you're a journalist. You must know about it. Is there any law like that?"

Rajamanickam looked irked by the taunt. He turned to Thenmozhi. "Thenu, you go on. I'll talk to them," he said, uneasily.

She began to move away. As she left, she gave Rajendran a long look. She had met him first at the temple tank; seeing him here, for the second time, there was a flutter in her eyelashes. She walked off down the path between the fields with a noticeable sway in her hips.

Rudra, who was watching her carefully, suddenly called out to her. "Stop, ma!" he cried. Thenmozhi stopped, frightened, and turned to face Rudra. His eyes were on the diamond necklace around her neck.

"Come a little closer."

"Sir! Why are you calling her?"

"Wait a minute, Rajamanickam. What's around your neck? A necklace, is it?"

"Yes."

"It's shining like diamonds."

"It is d-d-diamonds." Thenmozhi's voice stuttered like a telegraph machine.

"You've come to the fields wearing a diamond necklace? You look like you've come to bathe."

Rudra had cornered her. In response, she looked at Rajamanickam. She quickly removed the necklace and put it in his hand. Eager to leave the scene, she turned to hurry home.

"What's the meaning of this, sir?" Rajamanickam hissed. "That's the girl I'm going to marry. I gave her this necklace as a token of love. Now after your interrogation, she's taken it off and run away!"

"Never mind all that. How did you get your hands on such an expensive necklace?" Rudra's question made Rajamanickam's face turn red. He re-folded his veshti around his waist and glared back at the police inspector.

"Don't look at me like that, Rajamanickam. I've come to meet you to make some inquiries."

"What sort of inquiries, sir? What have I done?"

"See how you're getting all worked up? Only a guilty person would start having palpitations like this."

"Go tell your stories to someone else. If someone starts falsely accusing you of wrongdoing, of course your heart will start pounding. You should know that."

"Okay, come. Let's go sit down over there and talk."

"I don't have time to sit and chat, sir. Get to the point. Why did you want to meet me?" Rajamanickam demanded, gesticulating angrily.

"Look, I'm a policeman. And you're someone who knows very well what policemen are like. I've given you a few beatings inside the lock-up at the Tirunelveli police station myself. Have you forgotten that?"

At Rudra's mention of the past, Rajamanickam seemed to soften. "What is it that you want me to do now, sir?"

"First, let's go over by the pump and talk. It's hot here."

Rudra got down from the ridge and began to walk ahead into the field. Rajendran and Rajamanickam followed him silently.

Gubbu gubbu! The water frothed milky white as it gushed out from the pump. Rajamanickam turned it off and chased away the kids who had been bathing there. There were a few workers scattered about the vicinity, weeding. Rajamanickam motioned for them to move further away. Many left, fearful. A few of them remained, though—out of earshot, but close enough to watch what was going on.

"*Apai!*" said one of the workers to the others. "Looks like Naicker's daughter's wedding is going to be cancelled once more. The police are digging into Rajamanickam's case again."

"That poor girl! I wonder what he's been up to this time," said another.

Rudra began his questions.

"Rajamanickam, before he chose you, hadn't Naicker decided on someone called Ganesan to be the mappillai?"

"Yes."

"You even filed a police complaint when that boy ran off with ten lakhs, didn't you?"

"Yes. Is that what you're here to investigate?"

"Not only that. A few days ago, a man called Ramasamy died in the village."

"Yes, the fellow who got struck down by the evil spirit."

"You say it was an evil spirit. We think it was a criminal."

"Okay, so what do I have to do with it?"

"We came to ask if you know anything more about it."

"Whenever something happens somewhere, do you have to come straight to me?"

"Where else should we go? I don't really have to elaborate who you are and what kind of a person you've proven yourself to be, do I?"

"Inspector sir, I might have been a rowdy once. But now I'm going to become this village naataamai's son-in-law. Don't come to me and stir up old rubbish!"

"'Are you saying that the old Rajamanickam is dead?"

"Yes."

"Fine, let's leave it. I just want to ask you one question."

"What?"

"They say that ghosts roam around that hill near the village. Is it true?"

Rajamanickam's anger flared. He shot bullets through his eyes at Rudra.

"What Rajamanickam, why are you staring at me like that?"

"Why don't you head over that way one night and have a look. Find out for yourself what's true and what isn't."

"I've already been there."

Rajamanickam hadn't expected this. He hesitated.

"What Rajamanickam, not able to believe it?"

"You're trying to trap me."

"Trap you, ah? You're the one who's the experienced trickster! Anyway, leave it. You're saying that spirits haunt the hill. That is your opinion, right?"

"Not just me, the whole village believes it. And I do too."

"Very good. We'll leave now." Rudra abruptly stopped talking and turned to look at Rajendran.

Rajamanickam was staring daggers at Rajendran, while Rajendran stared daggers back, the glares from their eyes jostling and colliding into each other.

* * *

Several police vans were parked near the canal bank.

It seemed like all of Aayakudi had gathered to watch the police. Everyone's eyes were focused on them as they climbed up and down the slope of the hill.

One policeman carried four or five skulls in his arms, as if they were a bunch of coconuts, and placed them by one of the vans. Another brought down a variety of bones, each from a different body part.

Two panting police dogs leaped around the area. One of them began digging with its front paws at a particular spot next to the canal. It was the same spot where Rajendran had stuck his pen as a marker the previous night. The dog had the pen in its mouth.

Rajendran and Rudra arrived just at the right time. The policeman who was with the dog took the pen from its mouth and showed it to Rudra.

"What, ya?" asked Rudra.

"Sir, we've searched the entire area. There's no one here sir. But we found many skulls and bones—very old ones. Our dog Rita thinks there's something suspicious right here where we're standing. She found this pen."

"Sir! That's my pen!" exclaimed Rajendran. Rudra looked at him curiously.

"Last night, as I stood on this spot, I felt a tremor. Because it was dark, I stuck my pen in the ground so that I'd be able to identify the place in the morning." Rudra looked at Rajendran, thinking. Then he asked the policemen to dig up the ground in that spot at once. They began, working at a furious pace. Rudra moved towards the police van to look at the skulls. Rajendran followed him.

"Rajendran."

"Sir."

"Did you study the way Rajamanickam was acting?"

"I did, sir. But I didn't see any sign of fear or panic, or any indication of guilt. Instead he only showed anger."

"I expected that. In fact, it looks like Rajamanickam did not have the opportunity to commit these crimes."

Rudra's answer made Rajendran think.

"What, Rajendran, you're wondering how I came to that conclusion?"

"No sir, if you say so it must be right. Still, isn't there a possibility that Rajamanickam's fooling us—that he's just a very talented actor?"

"Certainly. Just because I think that way doesn't mean I'm letting him off the hook entirely."

"But according to you the criminal is someone else?"

"It has to be."

"What about what Ramasamy's ghost said when it entered me... and everything Ganesan's ghost said when it entered Pechi?"

"You know very well that none of this ghost business holds any weight anywhere. Why do you keep bringing it up?"

"I don't expect to go to court with it, sir. Just between us."

"I'm sorry, Rajendran. When the spirit who spoke to you comes and speaks to me, then maybe I'll consider it."

"But you didn't try becoming a medium the way I did. So how could you know?"

"I have a lot of questions about becoming a medium. If there really were spirits, I can't believe they'd come to us complaining and moaning this way. I imagine they'd take things into their own hands, deal with the criminals on their own. Now that's the kind of spirit whose actions and existence I could probably come to terms with."

"Then what about *my* experience as a medium?"

"Couldn't it have all just been in your mind?"

"What about the experiences we *both* had, last night, at this very spot?"

"Don't you think it could have been a show put on by the criminals to scare us into running away?"

"You're still convinced that spirits, ghosts, and demons are all imaginary?"

"Definitely. The only thing certain here is that an escaped convict is dead. I think the criminals are using these old bones and false stories about spirits haunting this hill to take advantage of the villagers' superstitions and commit one crime after another."

"That may be so, sir. But what about that voice that I heard? And the tremors I felt?"

"Very simple. That voice came from someone who was hiding nearby. As for the shaking ground—it could just be remotely controlled machines!"

"So, you're convinced these criminals are behind it all? No room for anything supernatural?"

"One hundred per cent!" Rudra said firmly.

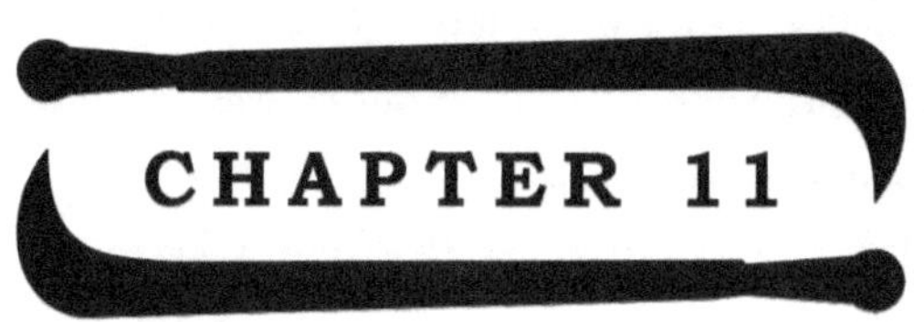

CHAPTER 11

After digging for a while, the police found the convict's corpse.

The face was badly mangled. It looked as if it had been smashed in with a rock. Rudra leaned over to look and quickly pulled his head away, unable to bear the stench.

Rajendran, with his handkerchief tied around his nose, peered in to look. He grimaced.

He was still wearing his prison clothes, now tinted a light orange from the red soil that covered the area. There did not seem to be any damage to his arms or legs.

"Sir... when we saw this body on the rock, the face was undamaged. But now it's crushed beyond recognition. Isn't that right sir?" Rajendran asked, slipping into the role of a journalist again.

"Yes, you're right. Also, how did they manage to get the body down from the rocks so quickly and bury it here? That's the main question," said Rudra.

"And why did they have to mutilate his face?"

"They've got us running in circles, don't they?"

"I feel like tearing my head apart!"

"Well, if this is the first time that investigating a news story has made you feel that way, thambi, just imagine the life of a policeman. This is what we have to deal with twenty-four hours a day!"

As they spoke, the body was lifted onto a stretcher and readied to be taken for a post-mortem.

It was a sign of modern times that one policeman was capturing everything on a video camera. From digging the pit, to pulling out the body, to the entire post-mortem procedure, everything was recorded— no matter how long it took. Rudra implemented this practice in every case he oversaw; there were many different ways that having a full record on video could turn out to be helpful.

The residents of Aayakudi were watching from a distance. Their faces wore astonished expressions. Rudra walked slowly towards them. As he approached, some of them began to slink away.

"Stop!" ordered Rudra, in an intimidating voice. The villagers halted in their tracks, fear in their eyes.

One of them, a man in a lungi, spoke up. "*Saami*, we don't know anything. So many of you policemen showed up all of a sudden... we just came to see what was happening, that's all!" he said timidly.

"Your name?"

"Mayavan, sir."

"What do you do?"

"Aiyya, I work in the fields."

"You're a native of this village?"

"Yes sir. My family has been here for many generations."

"Have you been out by the hill recently?"

"Aiyyo! No one goes that side. That's where the evil spirit roams."

"Since when?"

"Since as far back as I can remember."

"So no one *ever* goes there? Not even a fly, or a crow?"

"It's not like that, sir. One in a while our cows and goats wander off that way. Then we have to pray to Ayyanaar, smear ourselves with vibuthi, sing loudly, and try to herd our animals back."

"But you've never seen anyone there?"

"I haven't, sir."

"I heard that Naicker's son-in-law Rajamanickam used to go there," Rudra remarked calmly, as though threading a needle and slowly pulling on the string.

"Aiyyo! I never saw him!"

"Don't lie!"

"I swear!"

"Don't be afraid. No harm will come to you from Rajamanickam. I will guarantee that."

"No sir! I've never seen anyone out on the hill, so how can I lie and tell you that I have? Aiyya, just let me go now!" he pleaded. "I'll... I'll take your leave." And with that he ran away.

Rajendran looked on silently. Another member of the crowd looked as if he was weighing whether or not come forward and say something. Rudra noticed him, and called him over with a snap of his fingers. The man came closer. His mouth was full of Pan Parag and his face stank of it. On his feet were a pair of brand new Ceylon chappals.

Rudra sized him up. "What, man? If you've got something to say, say it."

"I'll tell you, but you have to ask first."

"Well, I'm listening– talk."

"I can't just talk. You have to ask me questions."

"What are you blabbering?"

"You know, like 'Is Rajamanickam an upstanding fellow? What kind of a person is he?'... Ask me one by one."

He went on chewing Pan Parag the whole time he talked. Rudra's stare pierced through him.

"Okay. Why the fancy footwear?"

"Well, they're new. So, they look new."

"That's not what I mean. Those are some unique chappals. Not something you usually see in a village like this. That's why I asked."

"What, sir! Here I am expecting you to ask about Rajamanickam, and instead you're asking about my chappals!" he responded indignantly. "What next? Are you going to ask what brand they are? How much they cost? Where I bought them?"

Rudra felt like taking the chappals and giving the man a good whack with them. "Okay, fine," he said. "What kind of a person is Rajamanickam?"

"The whole village knows he's a villain."

"Oho. Okay. Does he ever visit that hill?"

"Does he ever visit? Every night around nine o'clock he heads off that way with a bottle in his hand. There's a cave up there. Go inside and look—you'll see it's full of bottles. Once in a while he takes girls there too. What to say! Full enjoyment!"

"Have you seen all this yourself?"

"I wouldn't say so if I hadn't."

"Your name?"

"Mariadas."

"You're from this village?"

"Where else?"

"How come you're coming forward so boldly and talking about Rajamanickam?"

"Well, I figure you're going to catch hold of him and put him in jail whether I speak to you or not. So what exactly do I have to fear?"

"Looks like you've made up your mind he's the person responsible."

"Sir! Ramasamy's ghost itself told you that he's the guilty one. What's wrong with me coming to the same conclusion?"

Narukku! Rudra felt like he'd just cracked his tooth on a stone.

"Okay, how did you know that the ghost came and spoke to us?"

"The teacher was talking about it."

"Oho," said Rudra, arching an eyebrow.

"Sir, enough talk. First go and put that Rajamanickam in jail. Otherwise he'll commit another murder and make you run around even more."

Mariadas continued to speak arrogantly, without a drop of fear. He opened another sachet of Pan Parag in front of Rudra.

"That stuff has been prohibited by law, did you know that?"

"The law also prohibits policemen from beating their prisoners. Did that ever stop you?'

He put all of the Pan Parag in his mouth in one swift motion and began to chew as he walked back into the crowd.

For some time, Rudra trained his gaze on him. Rajendran came to his side slowly.

"Sir."

"Hmmmm?"

"I feel like there was something insincere about the way he was talking."

"I thought the same! He's deliberately targeting Rajamanickam. My theory is getting stronger and stronger."

"What do you mean?"

"All I'll say for now is this: I feel sorry for Rajamanickam."

"Sir!"

"Yes, Rajendran—I think there's a big conspiracy underway here. Every single step is being planned and orchestrated."

Rudra walked away and stood by himself under a nearby tree.

The van carrying the convict's corpse had just started off. Rudra waved it onwards from where he stood. Speaking on his cell phone to someone inside the vehicle, he gave the order: "Make sure the post-mortem is carried out with utmost care!" and then proceeded to call the superintendent of the Palayamkottai prison.

"Superintendent sir, this is Inspector Rudrapathy from Crime Branch. I'm calling from Aayakudi."

"Tell me Rudra, what can I do for you?"

"I want some information from your files on that escaped prisoner of yours, Irumbaadi. Specifically, if there are any marks on his body."

"It sounds like you've found an unidentified corpse somewhere."

"Pretty much sir. I would also like to inform you—unofficially of course—that it is possible that Irumbaadi has been murdered."

"What? Irumbaadi's been killed?"

"Yes. The body's just been sent for post-mortem. His face was disfigured beyond recognition, so we need to check if any of the marks mentioned in your file are present on the body."

"I'll have Xerox copies sent across immediately."

"Don't bother with Xerox copies sir. Just take a look at the file and tell me over the phone itself."

"Give me an hour. I'm in my quarters right now. Let me get to the prison, hunt down that file, and call you back when I have it in my hands."

"Thank you very much, sir."

Rudra finished talking and looked up. Rajendran's eyes were fixed on him.

"What, sir? Now you're doubting the identity of the corpse we found?"

"Yes, Rajendran. Now stop asking me questions. Take a look at what's coming."

Rajendran looked in the direction that Rudra was pointing. Rajamanickam, Govinda Naicker, and a few others were walking furiously towards Rudra.

"See, Rajendran," Rudra said quietly. "Do you think someone who is actually guilty would be so brave as to march right up to the police like that?"

As they got closer, Naicker brought his hands together in a polite greeting. His face was a mix of anxiety, fear, and anger.

"Vanakkam, sir!" Naicker started off.

"Vanakkam. I was about to go call on you, but you came to me first." Rudra's voice, too, was polite.

"What's going on here in our village, sir? We're just simple people who mind our own business. This is the first time in my life I've seen the police even set foot here. We've always managed to settle our issues amongst ourselves." Naicker sounded very worried as he spoke.

Rudra smiled.

Naicker continued, "It seems you've put my son-in-law here through a lot of questioning. He expressed his disappointment to me."

"What can I say sir? I have to carry out my duties."

"Oh, certainly! Please, execute your duties to the fullest. My concern is just this: as the village panchayat president, I'm not even aware of what crimes have taken place."

"That's surprising! Not just one, but three murders have taken place here. And you say you know nothing?"

"Murder? Here in our village?"

"This area—the hill and the canal—all comes within the boundary of your village, doesn't it?"

"Yes, of course. But who has killed whom?"

"Ramasamy is dead, and all of his funeral rites have been performed, isn't that right?"

"Yes, but what of that now?"

"The information we have is that he was murdered.""

"*Adi aathi!* He had an encounter with an evil spirit and died of fright. Didn't he?"

"That is your opinion. Unfortunately, his body has already been cremated. Otherwise the truth might have come out in the post-mortem."

"Well, suppose that's one. Who are the other two?"

"One is Ganesan, who people say cheated you and ran away with ten lakhs of your money. The other is an escaped convict named Irumbaadi."

"What! Ganesan was murdered?!"

"That's the information we have. But we are still looking for his body."

"And the convict?"

"We found his corpse. It's been sent for post-mortem."

"How tragic! I can't believe it. I was told that Ganesan had made his way to Bombay."

"That may have been what you were told. But it isn't necessarily the truth."

"I suppose that's possible. How can there be so much going in this village without my knowledge? Ayyanaare!" Naicker looked devastated as he dabbed at the perspiration around his neck.

Suddenly there was an outburst from Rajamanickam. "Who gave you all of this information? How do you know any of it is true?" As he asked these questions, he was looking straight at Rajendran.

"Why are you staring at him?" asked Rudra. "He's a journalist. He has a lot more freedom than I do—I don't believe that I am under any obligation to tell you where we got our information from."

"How is that possible? Govinda Naicker here is the village panchayat president. Shouldn't he be kept updated on what's going on?"

Rajamanickam had posed a fair question, but Rudra didn't seem perturbed by it. He just smiled lightly and said nothing.

"I know what this is all about, sir," Rajamanickam went on. "It's all that teacher's doing. One day I slapped him when I was drunk. That was a mistake, and I regret it greatly now. But he's still nursing a grudge, and he's instigated all of you against me." This introduced a completely new angle to the issue. Rudra's ears perked up.

"Rajamanickam, forget about what the teacher did or didn't say. There was a guy named Mariadas here just now. He told us a few things about your activities around this area. What do you have to say about that?"

"Mariadas?" said Rajamanickam, shocked. "Who's that, sir?"

"He was just here," said Rudra, looking around in the crowd for him. But Mariadas was nowhere to be seen.

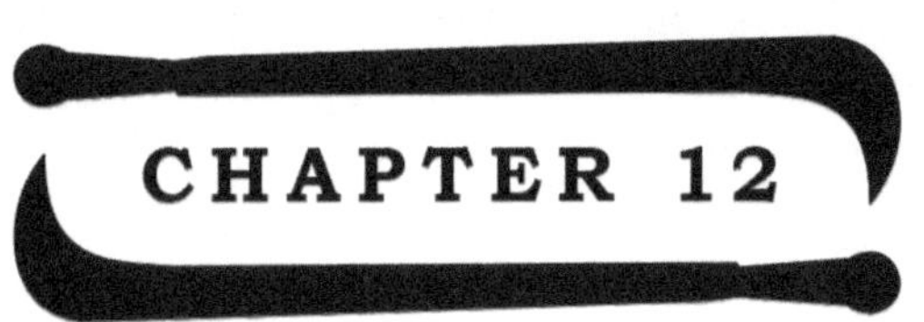

CHAPTER 12

RAJAMANICKAM WAS HOPPING WITH RAGE; it looked as if he might jump up to the sky and back.

"Where is this Mariadas, sir? Call him here. If he has any guts, let him look me in the eye and accuse me. Where is he? Where is he, sir?"

Rudra quickly tried to placate him. "Rajamanickam, he was just here a moment ago. I think he snuck away when he saw you. How does it matter if he is here or not? To policemen like us, information is what matters."

"Listen," Naicker cut in, irked. "My future son-in-law here might have done wrong in the past. But he's a changed man now. If he were still involved in criminal activities, why would I agree to get him married to my daughter?" he asked forcefully.

"I applaud your faith in him. But I am only doing my duty."

"Your sense of duty is going to impact my daughter's life. If one more wedding falls through, I am certain she will kill herself." Naicker's eyes began to tear up.

This affected Rudra too. He patted Naicker encouragingly on his shoulder. "You take care of the wedding arrangements. We'll take care of capturing the criminals."

His words implied that Rajamanickam was no longer on his list of suspects, and Naicker seemed to understand.

Rajendran was in the teacher's backyard washing his shirt and trousers near the well. It had been a few days since he'd arrived in Aayakudi; he was still trying to make sense of everything that had happened. At first, he had planned on writing a thrilling, fast-paced, multi-part series featuring evil spirits. Somehow, that no longer seemed like the right approach.

He had placed his cell phone on a small cement slab nearby. Its ring called out to him. He picked it up with wet hands. On the other end was his editor.

"Vanakkam, sir."

"Let's dispense with the pleasantries. What are you up to?"

"Carrying on sir. I just washed my clothes and put them out to dry. I have to go take a bath next."

"So, are you standing by the banks of a river or a pond right now?"

"Neither sir. I'm at Deenadayalan's house."

"Sounds like you've set up a permanent camp there. How are things progressing?"

"They're going on, sir."

"I'm sure they are. Tell me where they stand right now. Why are you like a stone that's been dropped into a well? Can't you move things forward?"

"That's a very accurate description sir! It's not just me... nobody around here seems to understand what's going on. Even Inspector Rudra is scratching his head trying to make sense of the situation."

"So, for the moment, you've got nothing concrete in hand."

"I do have something, sir. There's a murderer around for certain. And he's doing a very good job of hiding from the police. The trouble is in finding out where he is."

"So, all of that talk of ghosts and spirits has come to naught, then?"

"That's what Inspector Rudra says. He thinks this is all a well-planned drama that someone's staging."

"Isn't that how it always turns out? Why do you need him to explain that to you?"

"Sir, if it wasn't for his involvement, I would certainly have started believing in the existence of spirits, and that all of this was their handiwork!"

"Okay, give me a quick summary."

"Three people have been murdered. But hardly anyone in Aayakudi knows about it yet. The village hasn't even been affected much. The convict isn't from around here, and the other two deaths are only murders if we believe the ghost's testimony. The police are unwilling to accept that version, and the village doesn't know any better either."

"This is a very unique case indeed."

"It certainly is, sir. Usually there's an affected party seeking justice, and doing whatever they can to get it. But none of that is true here. At first we suspected that convict, but that was about it."

"There is still an angle to be pursued—who killed the convict?"

"Correct. That's what Inspector Rudra is following up on; that's his assignment henceforth. In fact, I'm not too sure that I have too much left to do out here anymore."

"So, are you planning on coming back?"

"Yes sir. Maybe I can write about how I was conned into all of these experiences with spirits. According to Rudra, this is a murder case now, nothing supernatural about it."

"Okay. Make it back in good time—there are a lot of papers piling up on your desk. At least you aren't coming back empty-handed; you can write a story about the escaped convict and how he died."

"Alright sir. Let my clothes dry out. The train leaves tonight. I'll see you at work in the morning."

Rajendran finished talking and put the phone away. He turned to see the teacher watching him, his eyes tinged with sorrow.

"What? Were you listening to me talking to my editor?"

"Yes, thambi. Are you leaving tonight itself?"

"I am. What's left for me to do here?"

"I suppose that's a valid question. The matter is now in the hands of the police. Anyway, it looks like some good will come of your visit here: if they do catch the killer behind it all, people might start being less super-stitious about ghosts and spirits. That much is very heartening!"

"I'll be glad of that too," said Rajendran. "But something is still nag-ging at me."

"What is that, thambi?"

"Your naataamai Govinda Naicker's daughter. Will her wedding still take place?"

"Rudra himself told him to go ahead with the arrangements. Why worry about that?"

"He might have said that just to calm him down. Rajamanickam is a convicted felon, after all. Surely he'll remain a suspect until they catch somebody else."

Rajendran's statement got the teacher thinking as well.

* * *

Thenmozhi sat on the floor. The room was dark, save for a bit of light from the evening sun trickling in through the window. She could hear her parents talking about Rajamanickam just outside the room.

"I don't know what cursed hour it was that you gave birth to this child! Every single time the topic of her marriage comes up, a new obsta-cle crops up out of nowhere!"

"I don't understand it either. Fate doesn't seem to want to let go—even after we've stooped so low as to select my thief of a brother as the groom."

"He goes on and on like a broken record, 'Maama, I've turned over a new leaf. I'm on the straight and narrow path now.' I'm not sure if I should believe him anymore!"

"Maybe we should postpone things for a while. I don't see how it could hurt?"

"Oh get lost, you senseless woman! Don't you remember what the astrologer said? If she doesn't get married in the next eleven days, she'll spend her whole life a spinster!"

Her father's warning—and her mother's silence that followed it—made tears roll down Thenmozhi's cheeks. She remained seated on the floor for a long while. Finally, she came to a decision. She quietly slipped out of the room and made her way to the back of the house and into the fields. She kept glancing over her shoulder as she walked away from the house. Then she stopped near a tree.

I'll surely marry you. And I won't take a single paisa from your father for it. My body is strong and my heart is bold. I'll take care of you like a queen. You're a lucky girl, Thenmozhi. Don't worry.

It was under this very tree that Ganesan had spoken those brave words to her.

But now there were two conflicting stories about her last would-be husband. Rajamanickam had told her Ganesan was somewhere near Bombay. But she had also overheard Rudra talking to her father, telling him that Ganesan had been killed.

I really have no luck, she thought.

The tree brought back more memories of Ganesan, pushing her deeper into sorrow.

She came to an abandoned well and looked down at the mossy sides, the green, spoiled water. It was a well in which several people were said to have drowned themselves. That was why no one used the water anymore, not even to irrigate their fields.

Just as she was mentally preparing herself to jump into the well and bid farewell to life, she heard a voice.

"Akka!"

She turned, and was shocked to see Ramasamy's daughter Chinna Pechi standing there. Pechi's eyes stared at her sharply, unblinking.

CHAPTER 13

THE GIRL WORE A STAINED cotton skirt and a half-sleeve jacket. Her hair was dishevelled. She looked a little like a doll made of mud.

Thenmozhi walked away from the well and towards Chinna Pechi.

"What, Akka? Are you going to die?" There was something menacing about her thin, unnaturally calm voice.

"P-Pechi... why are you here?"

"Why shouldn't I be here?"

"I mean how did you know *I* was here?"

"There's not much that escapes my notice, Thenmozhi. I'm a restless spirit, wandering all around the village."

Chinna Pechi was speaking with what sounded more and more like a male voice... One that Thenmozhi recognized.

"What are you staring at, Thenmozhi? It's me, Ramasamy."

"R-Ramasamy *Anna*?"

"Yes. The same Ramasamy who toiled hard in your fields."

"But, Anna... how are you here?"

"You've heard the stories of King Vikramaditya, where people would transition from one physical body to another, haven't you? I've come here in a very similar fashion."

"Anna!" Thenmozhi's body began to tremble. Small beads of sweat formed all over her skin. She was very visibly scared.

Dusk was falling and it was getting dark. A small dragonfly fluttered about, arcing and meandering through the sky—a sign that it was about to rain.

"Don't be scared Thenmozhi. You are like a daughter to me. I've only come here to help you."

"Anna… I mean, Pechi…"

"I'm not Pechi. I'm Ramasamy. My poor daughter—I have abandoned her."

"Anna... What you are saying?"

"I haven't said anything yet."

"Wh-what are you trying to say?"

"Just this: Don't kill yourself. If you do, then you'll end up like me, wandering around for eternity, never finding peace."

Thenmozhi was silent.

"Don't you believe me?"

"Anna, I think wandering around as a spirit might be better than living this cursed life."

"Don't speak like a mad person. And don't worry—you'll most certainly get married. But that's not the most important issue now."

"What are you talking about?"

"Listen to me carefully, Thenmozhi! There have been three murders so far in Aayakudi—and there are six more murders yet to come."

"Anna!"

"Don't panic. Go and tell the policeman what I said. Tell him the convict is still alive. If you want to know more, all you need to do is—"

Suddenly, as though someone had changed the channel on a television set, Pechi's personality switched.

"Akka! Thenmozhi Akka… how did I get here?" The male voice was gone.

Thenmozhi's head was spinning with questions. What had happened to the Ramasamy she'd just been talking to? What had he been about to say? Why couldn't he finish saying it? Had his spirit left Chinna Pechi's body for good?

"Akka, I'm feeling really scared. Aiyyo! We're here by the ghost well! Akka, come let us get away from this place." Chinna Pechi started walking away, and Thenmozhi followed her.

Ramasamy's words coiled around her mind, gripping her like a snake with its hood spread out.

Six more murders yet to come…!

* * *

Rajendran was carefully folding and packing his clothes in his bag. The teacher watched him closely.

The clock showed seven.

"What time is the last bus, sir?"

"It must be on its way right now, thambi. If you leave now, you should make it."

Rajendran picked up his bags. Then he remembered his phone and charger, and stuck both into his leather waist pouch. He looked up at the teacher, grateful.

"I can't quite explain it, thambi. But I have this confusion in my head."

"Why sir? You don't want me to leave?"

"You can't put it that way. But these four-five days that you've spent here—I'll never forget them."

"Same here, sir. This village still has a long way to catch up with the modern world. But knowing that there are people like you living in places like this gives me great hope."

"I'm happy to hear you say it, thambi. Now you must get going."

Rajendran put on his backpack and stepped out of the house.

A distant streetlight illuminated the path ahead. A stray dog ambled across. The quietness of the night was interrupted by the sound of a cow urinating nearby.

He turned around. "I'll make a move, sir."

"I hope to see you soon. You should visit this village again."

"Surely sir. I will be back."

"Please don't forget to write about the poor condition our roads are in. And how we don't have access to good water."

"I will," said Rajendran, and began walking.

The stray dog trotted alongside him. He came to a stretch of road that was covered in slush. It didn't look like he could walk through it without getting very muddy. The sky was darkening, too.

Nearby, an old man was lying on a cot laid out on the street. He looked at Rajendran and said, "Go around to where the fields are, then keep heading east. You'll reach the tar road. You can flag the bus down there."

He thanked the kind-hearted villager who proffered his help without even being asked for it and headed in the direction he had indicated. The dog followed him, like an obedient servant behind his master.

The fields had just been harvested and the produce lay in piles on the ground. He tripped over one of them. Watching his steps more carefully, he made his way across the field. The dog ran ahead.

Suddenly he heard the dog barking.

Rajendran turned in the direction it was facing. He could see two thin, black figures walking towards him. It was too dark to make out who they were. The dog barked even louder, surprising Rajendran with its sudden fierceness.

As the two black forms came closer, he realised it was Thenmozhi and Chinna Pechi.

The dog looked ready to pounce on Pechi. But the small girl stared back at it, her face burning with the same intense expression it had worn before.

Thenmozhi looked at her, shocked. Until a moment ago, Pechi had been telling her how scared she was, saying she wanted to go home. Now she was fearlessly staring down an agitated dog.

"Shoo! Go away! Go now…" Rajendran said, stepping in between them. Abruptly Pechi broke away and ran towards her house.

Thenmozhi, though, stayed where she was. Her eyes did not leave Rajendran. That look had quite an effect on him, too.

She was the first to speak. "You are…?

"Rajendran. I'm the sub-editor for *Selvam* magazine. You must have heard of it?"

"Mmm… yes. It's a good thing I met you out here. I have no idea what's going on." She paused, looking at his bags. "It looks like you're going back home?"

"Yes." As he nodded in assent, he could see the headlights of the bus coming around a curve on the tar road. The light from the headlights jumped through the little gaps in between the thick leaves of a nearby tamarind tree.

"My bus is here. I'm leaving now. Was it something important?"

She saw the bus too and said, "Yes. It is really important. But I am not sure to what extent you will believe me."

"Why don't you tell me what it is first and then I'll let you know."

"Yes, I'll tell you. So far, this village has seen three killings. There are apparently six more deaths yet to come. Ramasamy's ghost entered the body of Chinna Pechi, that girl who just ran away, and told me all about it…" She paused. "Just as I was about to commit suicide."

These last words left Rajendran frozen in shock.

The bus had dropped off its passengers and was getting ready to leave. Just then, the rain began to fall.

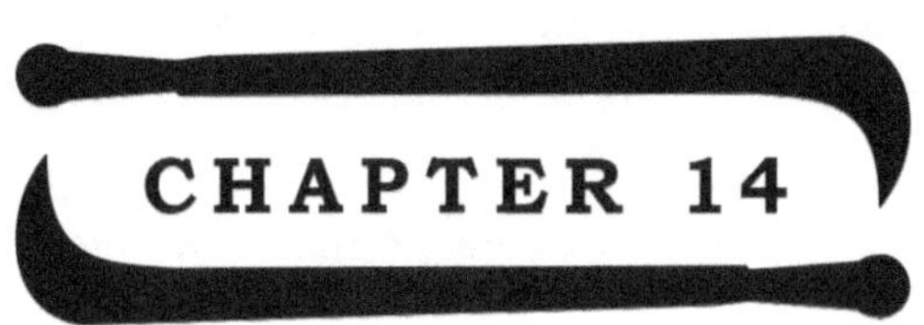

CHAPTER 14

It was coming down heavily. The bus had departed. Darkness enveloped Rajendran and Thenmozhi as both of them began looking around for a place to seek shelter. When a bolt of lightning lit up the sky, they glimpsed a small hut and a haystack nearby.

Rajendran ran quickly towards the hut. Thenmozhi, not sure what else to do, followed him.

The door of the hut was unlocked. Inside was a small earthen lamp. In the corner was a cot, and on the cot was an old lady.

They both ran inside to get out of the rain. Thenmozhi, wiping her face with the edge of her sari, caught sight of the old lady and let out a deep breath.

"We've barged into this woman's home and she isn't even saying anything," Rajendran whispered, watching her. "Do you know her?"

"Yes. This is Ramayee. She's blind and deaf. She has a daughter—but she doesn't seem to be here now. That was the last bus, and she wasn't on it. Maybe she missed it and she's walking home."

"In a way this is a very good place for us."

Thenmozhi gave him a surprised look.

"Oh, don't misunderstand me. What you just told me outside is something extraordinary. I am not sure what to make of it. I just meant that this is a good place to continue our conversation."

"Oh! I thought you meant something else…" Her chest heaved, and then she relaxed.

"You're sure there are no more buses? That's it for the night?"

"Yes."

"Looks like I won't make it back to Chennai then. But that's okay. I thought my work here was done—but going by what you've just said, it sounds like there's still plenty to do!"

"I'm scared. Why is all this happening to me? I don't understand it."

"Be brave. Tell me what happened with Chinna Pechi."

"She started speaking in Ramasamy Anna's voice. Even thinking about it now makes my insides shake!"

"I wonder why all the ghosts only seem interested in possessing *her*."

"What do you mean, *all* the ghosts?"

Rajendran wasn't sure how to respond to the question. He didn't know if he should tell her about Ganesan's spirit communicating through Pechi.

His hesitation grated on her. "Did you speak to spirits through Pechi as well?" she asked.

"Yes!"

"Whose ghost did you talk to?"

"Oh, why go into all of that now? All this 'spirit' business… Inspector Rudra is sure it's all some sort of trickery. That's what I thought at first too. But now—especially after what you've just told me—I don't know what to believe anymore."

"Ramasamy Anna asked me to pass on some information to the police. But his spirit left abruptly, mid-conversation. Then Pechi started crying and talking in her own voice, asking to leave."

"What did Ramasamy ask you to tell the police?"

"He said that the dead body wasn't the escaped prisoner. That's one thing I remember for sure…"

"That would mean that the convict is still very much alive!"

As Rajendran said this, the rain poured down even harder. A deafening clap of thunder sounded out, as though the entire sky was a sheet of glass that had been shattered with a gigantic stone. The sound came from directly above them.

The loud noise startled Thenmozhi, pushing her into Rajendran's arms. She clung to him with the tight grip of a monitor lizard.

It was the first time she had ever held a man so closely.

Rajendran felt a surge of comfort from her touch course through him.

Through all this, Ramayee sat on her bed, pounding away at betel nuts in a small iron mortar. She was oblivious to the loud thunder and the pouring rain.

The two stood in an embrace for quite some time. Thenmozhi slowly loosened her grip and began to step back. Suddenly, overcome by embarrassment and guilt, she jumped back and stood a few feet away. Rajendran, too, slowly came back to his senses.

At that moment, his cell phone rang. He put it to his ear.

It was Rudra on the other end. "Rajendran, have you started for Chennai?"

"Yes sir. I was just about to call you myself. Good thing that you phoned."

"So that's it? Your investigation is over?"

"What kind of a question is that, sir? I'm not a policeman, you know; I can't spend all my days and nights trying to solve this one case. I've got other stories and essays to write."

"You have a good life, Rajendran! You can leave whenever you want to. But I think my work is only getting started."

"Have you received any new information?"

"You'll be amazed when I tell you what it is."

"I have some surprising news for you as well!"

"What is it, Rajendran? Did you meet Mariadas again?"

"No, no. Anyway, you tell me your news first."

"I will, but you have to promise not to publish it in your magazine yet. Also… I want you to postpone your journey. Stay on in Aayakudi for some more time."

"I think that'll be difficult, sir. My editor will tell me to quit my job as a reporter and join the police force instead!"

"No, he won't say anything like that. I've just spoken to him."

"Oh! So that's how it is. Don't you have enough people in your own department? Why are you asking me, a reporter of all people, to stay and help you?"

"For good reason Rajendran. Please."

"Okay, sir. But you still haven't shared your amazing news with me."

"The body we found—it's not Irumbaadi!"

Rajendran fell silent. Rudra's news was exactly what Ramasamy's ghost had told Thenmozhi! He turned to look at her.

"Rajendran, say something."

"Sir."

"What is it?"

"I was about to give you exactly the same bit of news!"

"About Irumbaadi? How did you come to know of it?"

"Well I'll say this much… You can't question the existence of spirits anymore, sir."

"What happened, Rajendran? You had another conversation with a ghost?"

"Not me, sir. Ramasamy's spirit possessed the body of that girl Chinna Pechi again. He said that the dead body wasn't the convict's—but he also dropped an even bigger bomb."

"What did he say?"

"He said that there were going to be six more murders in the village!"

"*What?*"

"I only heard the news ten minutes ago. I was on my way home, but because of this I missed my bus. Now I can't leave even if I wanted to."

Rajendran kept an eye on Thenmozhi throughout the conversation, but he carefully avoided mentioning her. She watched him too, surprised.

"But Rajendran, you said you didn't speak to the ghost. So, who did?"

"I'll explain in detail when we meet tomorrow, sir."

"Okay. I'll be at the teacher's house by eight tomorrow. Be ready."

"Yes sir!" Rajendran folded his phone and put it away in his pocket.

Thenmozhi's doe-like eyes still didn't leave Rajendran's face. The rain was not coming down so hard now.

"Was that the police?" she asked.

"Yes. So now they know, too."

"In all these years, this is the first time the police have come to our village."

"I wouldn't be surprised if they set up a permanent station here now. But let that be. Can I ask you something?"

"What?"

"What kind of a man is your soon-to-be husband, Rajamanickam?"

In an instant, her eyes were full of tears.

"What is it, Thenmozhi? Did I say something wrong?"

"Yes. Who told you that I was going to marry Rajamanickam?"

"The entire village is talking about it. Why, even your own father said so."

"Even if God himself comes down and tells me to do it, I will not marry that… thing. It's not even human. Just a beast. That's why I had decided to kill myself. But Chinna Pechi showed up and spoiled my plans."

"Is… is that how you met Pechi tonight?"

"Yes. Now everyone at home must be looking for me. If Rajamanickam catches me here with you, he won't wait for the wedding—he'll tie a thaali around my neck while I'm sleeping tonight and say that it's done! And before that, he'll chop you up into pieces!"

"Don't worry. You're not a minor, are you?"

"What do you mean?'"

"I mean, you're over 18, right?"

"Yes, I've had quite a few birthdays. In the month of *Aippasi*, I'll turn 26. My friend Raasaathi is the same age, and she has a son who's in the fifth standard!"

It was clear that despite her dissatisfaction with Rajamanickam, she was dreaming of a happy married life.

"Don't worry, Thenmozhi. No one can force you into a marriage against your will. I am here for you."

Thenmozhi looked at him, and ventured a smile. "So, you'll be staying here in our village a while longer, then?" she asked with a lilt in her voice.

"Yes. Now each day will bring a new thrill. Ghosts on one side, murderers on the other. I think I'm going to enjoy myself!"

"I'm still feeling scared."

"I'm here. Don't worry."

Rajendran had stopped addressing her formally; his words took on a greater sense of familiarity. It was a pleasant surprise for her as well. She gazed at him silently. He took a step towards her and snapped his fingers in front of her eyes. She slowly returned to her senses, embarrassed.

Just then, they heard someone at the door. They both turned to see who it was.

A furious Rajamanickam stared in at them.

"Aiyyo!" Thenmozhi's heart almost came to a stop. Rajendran, too, was frozen.

But Rajamanickam only stood there, watching them.

The seconds ticked on.

He didn't move.

Rajendran stepped forward. "What, Rajamanickam? Why so angry? Thenmozhi and I were just seeking shelter here from the rain."

But there was no response.

"Come on, say something. What happened to you?" Rajendran asked, nudging him lightly.

Rajamanickam fell forward like a tree trunk. His body was lifeless.

Lodged deep inside his back was a large knife.

CHAPTER 15

THENMOZHI COULDN'T EVEN MUSTER the strength to let out a scream. She ran and hid behind Rajendran. They were both too shocked to think clearly.

There was no noise from outside. Slowly regaining his faculties, Rajendran stepped over Rajamanickam and went outside the hut.

Darkness had constructed a nest around them. A couple of hens stirred. But there was no one else in sight. Rajendran couldn't understand how Rajamanickam had gotten there.

Had he been stabbed in the back after he had walked in? Or had he stumbled here with the knife in his back? A hundred questions criss-crossed his brain.

"Thenmozhi…"

"Mm-hmm…?"

"Make your way home at once. Don't breathe a word to anyone about coming here, about seeing me, or about seeing Rajamanickam's dead body. I'll inform Inspector Rudra. The first of the six deaths has already occurred; there are still five more to go. But we must do our best to stop them! That's on me, though… Come on, you have to leave this place now."

"What about you?"

"Don't worry about me. If anyone finds us here together, they could easily get the wrong idea."

"Fine. I'll leave."

"The most important thing is to keep this secret safely locked away. You mustn't get emotional and reveal what you saw here, even to your own parents. Don't tell anyone else about what you heard from Ramasamy's spirit, either. Listen to me carefully—*nothing happened to you*. You don't know anything. That's the story you have to stick to."

Rajendran's insistence made her pause.

"Thenmozhi, go. Please don't be worried. I'm here for you."

"What does that mean, you're here?"

"It means I'm here. I can't begin to understand your state of mind—but please, be brave. Don't... don't make any more rash decisions. I repeat, I'm here for you."

"No, Rajendran, don't say that. Ganesan said almost the exact same thing, and now he's gone; I don't even know what happened to him. Rajamanickam was madly attracted to me too, and he's dead as well. Now you..."

"Silly girl... I'm not like them. Nothing will happen to me. Even if something does, I know how to take care of myself. You go home now. This isn't the time to discuss all these things."

"Rajendran..."

"Swear to me that you won't breathe a word of this. Leave, now. And I give you my word—soon, you *will* be happily married."

Rajendran caught hold of her and pushed her in the direction of her house. She walked into the darkness, turning back every now and then to look at him.

Once she was out of sight, he walked away from the hut in the opposite direction.

Ramayee still hadn't moved from her cot.

* * *

Rainwater dripped down from the thatched roof. The frogs had started off their musical concert. Deenadayalan had rolled out his cot and was spreading a sheet over it. He turned around when he heard a street dog bark. Rajendran was walking back, his bag on his shoulders. He felt suddenly energized. "Thambi…"

"It is me, sir."

"Didn't you go home?"

"I missed the bus, so I turned back."

"How did you manage to miss the bus? I heard it come quite a while after you left here. I thought you'd be in Ambasamudram by now."

"No sir… I mean…" Rajendran's voice faltered.

"What, thambi? Is there some new mystery now?" the teacher guessed.

"Why don't we go inside and talk?"

Rajendran walked into the house with the teacher and bolted the wooden door behind them. The teacher made the round bulb come alive. Rajendran's face looked agitated in the dim yellow light.

"What, thambi? What happened?"

"Yes, aiyya… what shouldn't have happened has happened."

"What do you mean?"

"I'll tell you. But first I need to have a word with Inspector Rudra." Rajendran tried calling him on his cell phone. But the signal was very weak.

"These machines seem to know exactly when to let us down!" he said, irritated.

"What happened, thambi?" the teacher asked again. He was on edge as well, acting as jumpy as a severed lizard's tail.

Rajendran quickly narrated everything that happened, from the time he left the house to the time Rajamanickam fell dead at his feet.

The teacher looked broken, like a rock struck by lightning.

"Doesn't sound believable, no?"

"Not at all. Why is all of this happening? What's going on in this village?"

"And I think there's a lot more still to come. Just imagine that."

"You believe that there will be five more killings?"

"We can't allow them to happen. We need to figure out *why* these people are being targeted."

"My heart feels like it's about to stop. Imagine how dangerous a person must be if he's managed to kill someone like Rajamanickam!"

"Definitely. Listen, Rajamanickam's body is still in the hut. I walked away as if I didn't see anything. I asked Thenmozhi to leave as well."

"That was a good move. Poor girl though. What awful luck she's had!"

"Actually, sir, her luck isn't so bad at all. She's quite fortunate actually. You'll slowly come to understand that, I think."

"What are you saying, thambi?"

"Let's talk about her later. First, I need to inform Rudra. I also need to talk to my editor."

"Right. Please call Rudrapathy sir first. Let him get here. We need the police to occupy the village in force—otherwise we may lose five more lives."

With the teacher urging him on, Rajendran opened the door and stepped outside. He tried one more time on his cell phone. This time, the signal was strong.

"Sir."

"Tell me, Rajendran."

"Sir, come here immediately with all your troops. Something awful has just happened!"

"What is it?"

"Your hunch was right—Rajamanickam wasn't involved in those deaths."

"We already know that."

"Okay, but here's what you don't know: he's no longer alive."

Rajendran heard him gasp.

"It's true sir. I saw the body myself. Ramasamy's ghost predicted that there would be six more murders. This is the first of them."

"That's horrible. Who's behind it all?"

"Sir, I'm just a reporter. You're the one who needs to solve the case. Please come soon."

"It must be Irumbaadi's doing. I'm sure of it."

"Yes... Ramasamy's ghost mentioned that he was still alive."

"Oh, enough of your ghosts! I got a hold of Irumbaadi's prison file to match identifying marks on his body. The corpse with the mangled face—it's not him. He's killed somebody, put his own clothes on the body, and destroyed the face—all just to mislead us!"

"Sir... I understand why he might kill one person in order to escape. But why would he kill so many in a row? Why does he have to take nine lives?"

"That's a very good question. With a huge mystery behind it."

"You must leave at once, sir. Every minute you delay puts another life at risk."

With this urgent appeal, Rajendran put his phone away. He was suddenly reminded of Ramasamy's ghost.

"Teacher! I want to talk to the spirits again. Right now!"

"I thought you might! That seems to be our only way forward now," said the teacher, as he began making the arrangements.

"I know, I know—both body and mind need to be clean before I start. Wait, let me go wash up."

Rajendran changed out of his pants into a veshti and headed out to the well. He quickly washed his hands and feet and returned. He applied some sacred ash on his forehead and sat cross-legged on the floor. The teacher held out the notebook and pen. The night was quiet except for the croaking of the frogs. Rajendran calmed his mind and began focusing on a single point.

The teacher kept watching him. His unblinking eyes were focused on the pen to see if it would start writing.

Each second went past very slowly.
Suddenly, the pen moved!

I am very happy that you called me back, thambi. Tonight, I will tell you the cause behind all this strife. It is the treasure, dating from the times of Veerapandiya Kattabomman, that is buried there in the hillside.

With that, the pen paused. The teacher's eyes were anchored on the word "treasure".

CHAPTER 16

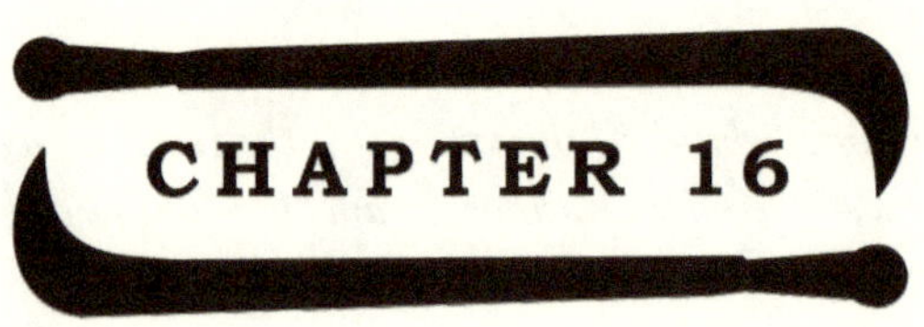

As DEENADAYALAN SAT TRANSFIXED, Rajendran's hand slowly began moving again.

There is a large hoard there, dating from the late 18th century. When Kattabomman's rebellion against the British East India company was defeated, after they captured and hanged him, his supporters didn't want his treasury's contents to fall into the hands of the white men. It is said that they divided up the wealth and buried it in multiple locations. One of those locations was here, at the hill in Aayakudi. But before anyone can possess the treasure, they need to perform a special sacrifice: they must perform eight murders, to gain control of the eight directions. Finally, as a ninth sacrifice, a virgin girl must be killed at the spot where the treasure is buried. Only then will the finder of the hoard be able to live in peace. This is the reason that lives are being taken around the village.

The person behind it, as you have guessed, is the convict Irumbaadi. The person who is guiding him is a sorcerer, a man well-versed in the lore of the treasure. This sorcerer is at this very moment somewhere here in Aayakudi. He brought Rajamanickam under his influence and demanded sacrifices. Rajamanickam wanted to marry Thenmozhi and run away from all of it, but the sorcerer had him firmly within his grasp—he cast a spell on him and controlled his actions. Rajamanickam killed me and Ganesan, but he didn't do so of his own accord. The sorcerer is the one responsible. Right now, he is itching to take control of both our spirits. The last time I spoke, he pulled me away with his sorcery. He now has complete command over Ganesan's spirit. So far I've managed to escape his clutches. I am glad that I have been able to tell the truth through you. Whatever comes next, I am not worried.

If I fail to show up the next time you call me, the sorcerer will be the one responsible for it. If anyone interferes in his hunt for the treasure, he'll do away with them and add them to his list of sacrifices. So you must proceed with caution—

The pen stopped abruptly. Rajendran's body jerked about. The pen slipped out of his hand, fell onto his lap and then rolled to the floor. Rajendran came back to his senses and looked at the teacher, who was staring at the paper.

"Thambi!"

"Aiyya…"

"Has the spirit left you?"

"Y-yes… Yes, aiyya."

"Then please read what you have written. My head is spinning."

Rajendran quickly read the handwriting in the notebook. "A treasure? *That's* what this is all about?"

"Thambi, even I have heard tales of Kattabomman's hoard of gold and diamonds. Then again, every village has stories of hidden treasure, so I never thought too much of it. But now…. it appears that this treasure is actually real!" said the teacher, in a hushed tone.

"So, you believe all this?"

"Don't you, after reading the notebook?"

"I'm a journalist. It's my job to question everything."

"Regardless of what your profession may be, don't your own experiences matter more?"

"Listen, let's get Rudra here. We'll dig up the whole hill and find the treasure."

"What is this, thambi? The treasure is not important right now. The important thing is to prevent any more deaths. Rudrapathy has to work to ensure that."

"You're right. Let Rudra sir get here. I don't think that this village is going to sleep easily any time soon," said Rajendran.

* * *

Thenmozhi sat shivering in one corner of the courtyard, like a white dove caught out in the rain. A few feet away were Naicker and Vanjiammal, seething with anger.

The pendulum clock on the wall, which seemed to have decided that its sole duty was to make some noise, went *troikkk, troikkk, troikkk* with each passing second.

A servant entered.

"*Dey*, what happened?" Naicker demanded.

"Sir, the astrologer wasn't at home. Apparently, he has gone to San-karankovil for some work. I have left word for him to come here as soon as he returns."

"Alright, you can go. As soon as that fellow comes back, I will insist that he make clear what this girl's future holds in store for her!" Naicker said as he brushed his greying moustache.

Vanjiammal was staring at a gecko on the wall.

Naicker spotted Thenmozhi as she walked back in from the rain.

"Where did you go off to, girl? Trying to kill us all off from worry?" he began shouting.

Thenmozhi kept mum, just as Rajendran had told her to. She wasn't going to utter a word about Rajamanickam's murder. Nevertheless, it was immediately obvious to Naicker that she had been somewhere she should not have been, and seen something she should not have seen.

Naicker's eyes kept going to the door. Thenmozhi that he was expecting Rajamanickam to come in at any moment. She couldn't reveal the fact that he was dead.

A cow kept mooing loudly in the backyard of the house. Vanjiammal figured someone must have forgotten to feed her oil cakes and grass. Finally, unable to bear the sound any longer, Vanjiammal headed to the back. As she got up, she glared at her daughter.

Thenmozhi put her head down and prayed to Lord Ganesha.

Vanjiammal's guess was right: the cow's trough was empty. She turned to fetch a sack of feed—and then stopped, surprised. The entire chicken coop was missing. There had been a couple of roosters, four hens and five or six chicks—all of them were gone! As she looked around for them, she saw someone standing at the edge of the back yard. Vanjiammal assumed that it was one of the workers.

"Hey! Who is that out there?" she called. "Mariappa? Periyasamy? What are you doing there at night? Where have all the hens gone?" She walked towards the figure. But as she got closer, the man jumped over the fence. She could see the hens fluttering in his hands.

A thief! Vanjiammal thought. The figure ran on, but he kept looking back at her, not watching where he was going. He ran straight into a big pile of stones and fell flat.

"Hey you scoundrel! Stop, thief!" Vanjiammal shouted. "Is anyone else around? Come quickly!"

She stepped under the fence and went out into the fields. As she approached the man lying near the stones and got a closer look at him, all of her senses went into shock!

He had wild, unruly hair and giant bulging eyes. His face was grotesque, terrifying.

He pushed her aside, threw the hens down, and began running.

The workers had heard the commotion and ran out to see what was happening, but they were too late. The man had escaped into the darkness; no one could make out where he was.

Naicker arrived as well.

"Hey pulla, what happened? Why did you shout? I thought I heard you shout at a thief."

"Yes but… the person I saw didn't look like an ordinary thief. He looked like a sorcerer."

"A sorcerer!"' Just as Naicker spoke, he heard engines. A police jeep and van, their headlights leaping about, roared up to his house. Thenmozhi peered out from inside and heaved a big sigh of relief.

Naicker walked up to the gate. The jeep stopped. Rudra jumped out and headed towards Naicker.

"What sir… at this hour?"

"Haven't you heard anything, Naicker?"

"I don't understand. What should I have heard?"

"Please come with us for a moment," Rudra said.

"Where to?"

"Just come. I came straight here after I heard the news."

Vanjiammal couldn't stop imagining all of the things that could have gone wrong for Rudra to show up at such a late hour.

Thenmozhi sat alone, watching everything quietly. The image of Rajamanickam lying in the hut with a knife in his back kept flashing before her eyes. Very soon, Vanjiammal would learn of his death, too. Thenmozhi thought about how badly her mother would be impacted by the news, how much she would cry.

"What are you talking about, sir?" said Naicker. "Just now some sorcerer has come and stolen our chickens, and run out of my house in that direction," he pointed. "And here you are calling me out *this* way. What is going on in this village?" he lamented.

"Hold yourself together. Come with me. You'll understand everything soon."

Govinda Naicker had no other option. He got into the jeep with Rudra and they drove away.

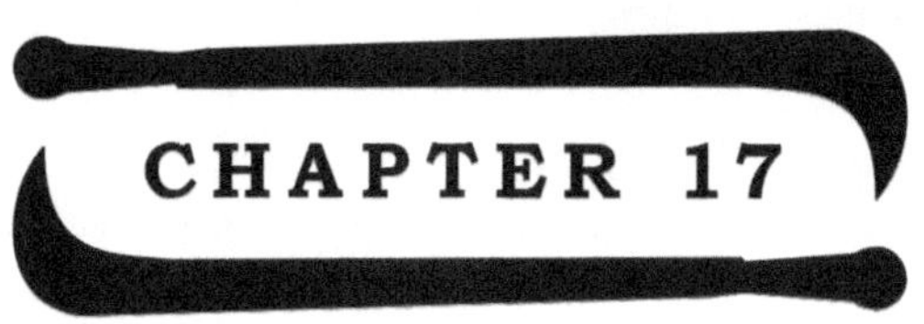

CHAPTER 17

RAJENDRAN LED THE WAY to the hut in the middle of the field. Rudra and a few more policemen accompanied him. Govinda Naicker walked beside them with his veshti hiked up. Several of the village folk watched from the edge of the field, astonished at the spectacle. A few of them held wooden torches.

"There, that's the hut," said Rajendran, pointing. One of the policemen shone the round light of his torch in that direction. In the light, one could make out a large haystack adjacent to the house. The hut was mushroom-shaped, made from dry corn stalks. As they got closer to the entrance, they could hear the old toothless lady still pounding at her betel nuts.

There was nothing else but the wet stickiness of the rain and the ongoing musical performance of the frogs.

Rajendran stepped up to the entrance and looked inside. The old lady was still sitting on her cot in the corner. The small oil lamp was still burning. And there was still no sign of the old lady's daughter.

But Rajamanickam's corpse was no longer in the place where it had lain!

Rajendran felt a sharp throbbing in his forehead. He stumbled back.

"What is it, Rajendran?" asked Rudra.

"The body is missing, sir."

"What? Missing?" Rudra leaned in to look.

Govinda Naicker stepped forward as well. "What is going on here? You aren't telling me a thing. You've brought me out to this hut and you're talking about a missing body. I don't understand a bit of it."

"Sir, we received news that your future son-in-law Rajamanickam had been killed, and that his body was lying in this hut. But there's no body here. I didn't want to tell you anything until I saw it myself. That's why…"

Rudra's quiet words shook Govinda Naicker.

"What!? Rajamanickam was killed? And his body is missing??"

"Yes sir… please don't get agitated."

"What, like this is some minor inconvenience? I was going to get him married to my daughter in ten days. And now you tell me he's dead!" Govinda Naicker exploded.

Instead of replying, Rudra turned to Rajendran.

"Sir. I swear that I saw Rajamanickam lying dead right here in this hut. Something has happened… after I spoke to you, but before we got here."

"Are you sure it was Rajamanickam? You got a good look at him?"

"Sir, please, you have to trust me. If you don't believe it you can—" Rajendran had been about to say "Ask Thenmozhi", but he quickly stopped himself.

"Come on! You were about to say something."

"Nothing, sir. I've told you what I saw. You know how shaken I was when I saw his body."

"Then the body has to be around here somewhere. Who would have stolen it? It's not like it's made out of gold or diamonds."

"I don't know sir. It doesn't make sense."

Throughout this animated discussion, the old lady stayed on her cot, pounding her betel nuts all the while—*nottu, nottu*—oblivious to the storm that was raging outside her door.

Govinda Naicker leaned on the haystack like a felled tree, unable to bear the thought that Thenmozhi's wedding would be called off yet again.

"Oh, my dear Thenu! What is the terrible fault in your stars? I have so much wealth, but I am unable to get you married. Who is the sinner being punished here? Is it you... or is it me?" he mumbled, bemoaning his fate. Rudra watched him, deeply affected by his words.

* * *

Dawn broke.

The astrologer was a passenger on board the first mini-bus of the day. As he got down at the Aayakudi stop, he was surprised to see policemen all around him. He stopped a local man.

"What is this, ya? Why are there so many policemen here? Is some minister visiting?"

"What do you mean! Haven't you heard that there's a killer out there who has struck terror into the hearts of the entire village? And here you are talking about ministers."

"A killer? In Rajamanickam's village?"

"It's not Rajamanickam's village anymore..."

"What are you saying?"

"The killer stabbed him to death, apparently. That's why all these policemen are here."

The astrologer felt like a woodpecker had pecked him hard on the top of his head. "Really?"

"Well, that's what they're saying. But they haven't found the body yet."

The astrologer spoke to a few other villagers and heard the rest of the rumours that were floating around. Then he began walking swiftly down the road.

Two dogs were approaching, their tongues hanging out, panting. Their police trainer was having trouble controlling them. They pulled him here and there as they zigzagged down the street. Right behind them were Rudra and Rajendran. The teacher was with them too, puffing a little as he tried to keep up.

The whole business seemed a great mystery to the astrologer. A pall of gloom had descended over the village.

One person ran into his home when he saw the dogs charging in his direction. A policeman noticed it, and dragged the man out and made him stand in front of the dogs. The man trembled. But the dogs quickly lost interest in him. He sighed in relief.

As the astrologer stood watching, one dog ran towards the canal. He was curious and wanted to follow the dog. But the image of Govinda Naicker in his head stopped him. The astrologer was sure, given everything that was happening around him, that Naicker would be in a panic. The best thing to do would be to go meet Naicker first. He began walking in the direction of his house.

Naicker was sitting on a chair just next to the grill gate. A crowd was gathered around him. On seeing the astrologer, the crowd parted slightly and made way.

"Aiyya—what is this? I am hearing so many things…" the astrologer asked as he approached Naicker.

Naicker didn't respond. He glared at him instead.

"Why are you looking at me like that? What did I do, aiyya?"

"How do you dare ask that, josiyare? You picked a wonderful date, that's what you did! Yet again, my daughter's wedding plans have ground to a halt!"

"No, no. My calculations are correct this time. Your daughter will get married on that day; I am certain of it."

"Enough! I've had enough of you and your astrology. I should have known that day itself, when the bottle gourd fell on your head. Just see what has happened? They can't even find my son-in-law's body!"

"Then, aiyya, what if that means Rajamanickam is still alive?"

"No. I can't hope for that. It's not just that reporter who saw him lying dead with a knife in his back. My own daughter has just admitted that she saw him as well."

On hearing those words, the astrologer turned to look at the window. Thenmozhi stood there, her face an emotionless mask.

"I can't believe it."

"I don't care what you can or can't believe. But don't you dare set foot in this village again with your stupid astrology!"

"Aiyya…"

"Get out of here this instant! Or in my current state of mind, I might just stab you to death! Run!"

The chickens in the yard started fluttering about, startled by Naicker's voice. The astrologer walked away with a sullen face.

As he walked down the dusty streets of Aayakudi, some people came running the other way. One of them bumped into the astrologer and fell down.

"Why are you people charging around blindly like this? Can't you see a man walking right in front of you?"

"They say they've dug up a bunch of corpses by the canal!" said the man who had fallen, getting up and running on. "Not a single one of them has a head!"

Shaken by this news, the astrologer too began running towards the canal.

Two corpses were laid out side by side. Both of them were headless. The policemen were digging up a third. Rudra and Rajendran were standing next to Rajamanickam's body, deep in discussion.

The police had fanned out across the hill, combing the whole area. The astrologer watched, not sure what to think. He walked towards Rajamanickam's body.

The well-built frame lay there on the ground, but no one knew where the head was.

The astrologer walked closer to the body and then quickly averted his face. He felt nauseous.

He asked a villager standing nearby. "Does anyone have an explanation for any of this?"

"It's the curse of the treasure."

"Treasure? What treasure?"

"Apparently, there's a huge treasure buried here. There's an escaped prisoner who's been eyeing it; he has a sorcerer as an accomplice. They require eight sacrifices—one for each of the eight directions—and then one more afterwards! Four sacrifices have been made already. There are five more left. I wonder who those five people will be!"

The man's story pierced the astrologer's heart. He even felt a little scared. Suddenly he decided he didn't want to stand there any longer, and began walking away quickly. He decided he would go back and see if the mini-bus had left yet. If it had… well, then he would just walk all the way back.

He reached the road in five minutes, but the bus was gone. So he started up the road.

After he had walked some distance from Aayakudi, he sat down under a tamarind tree to rest. It was an ancient, massive tree; its branches forked out in all directions. The leaves were lush and green after the recent rain.

From one of the branches, a figure with a soot-covered face was carefully watching the astrologer standing below.

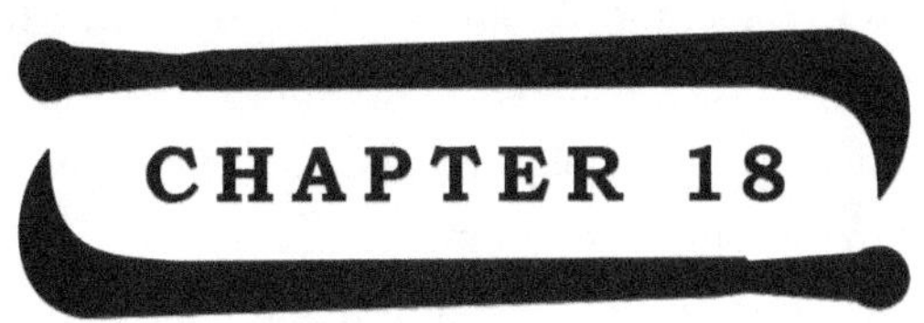# CHAPTER 18

Marthandam Pillai the Astrologer, unaware of the danger lurking overhead, let out a deep sigh. His neck was sticky with sweat. He towelled himself off while blowing some air to cool down. Then he thought he felt the tree branches shake, and he looked up.

He noticed the sorcerer hiding in the branches and his jaw dropped.

He wanted to say something, but the words wouldn't come out. The sorcerer jumped down—*soththu!*—onto the ground.

He had unkempt bushy hair, a moustache like the horns of a goat, eyes that were bulging and egg-shaped and smeared with kohl, yellowing teeth that seemed to grow in all directions, a necklace made of bones around his neck, dried blood spattered across his chest, a stomach like a round water pot, and a green belt holding up his black veshti.

The astrologer knew who he was.

"Aren't you the sorcerer Marnad?"

"Yes josiyare, indeed. It is me."

"Wh... what were you doing up there in the tree?"

"I was waiting for you."

"W-why?"

"The count is nine. One for each of the eight directions, and then the ninth must be a virgin girl. Of the eight, I'm already done with two—one sacrificed to Eesaanam in the Northeast, and another to Agni in the Southeast. I was just sitting here thinking about who I should sacrifice to Vayu in the Northwest—and here you are. The deity of my clan, Sudalamadan himself, has brought you to me!"

The astrologer cried out in a mix of fear and anger.

"Hush! Don't shout. You know I'm very capable of casting spells. If you try to escape, I'll tie up your legs and make you follow me."

"Marnad! No... please leave me alone."

"That I cannot. The next sacrifice must take place today. I have finished my prayers last night, before the transition to the next star sign."

"No Marnad! Please... I'm begging you. The police have gathered in large numbers in the village. I suppose you're the one who killed Rajamanickam. Naicker is extremely agitated. You won't be able to proceed. People know about the buried treasure—even I heard the talk. The police have surrounded the hill. How will you manage to go and retrieve it?"

"Who told you that there was a treasure buried in the hill?"

"Everyone was talking about it..."

"Good! Let them continue searching for it there. You come with me, now."

"Marnad... No! Leave me... please... Don't think that I will rat you out. I swear on my profession that I won't say a word to anyone!" the astrologer begged pathetically.

Marnad pulled out a bit of sacred ash from his waist. Disregarding the astrologer's pleas, the sorcerer mumbled something and blew the ash onto the other man's face.

A white cloud seemed to envelop the astrologer, and from then on, he did not open his mouth.

The astrologer followed Marnad like a calf behind its mother. They walked into a sugarcane field next to the road and disappeared.

* * *

A van was getting ready to take the headless corpses to Tirunelveli for the post-mortem. The local press had turned up in large numbers when they heard the news. Even TV reporters had arrived, with cameras in tow.

HUMAN SACRIFICE FOR HIDDEN TREASURE! screamed the headlines. *AAYAKUDI GRIPPED BY FEAR! WHO IS THE KILLER?*

A reporter was furiously typing out questions and sending out texts on his cell phone. Photographers were taking pictures of the hill from every possible angle.

Just then, a white Ambassador belonging to the Superintendent of Police made an urgent entry on to the scene.

Rudra ran up to the car and welcomed S.P. Chidambara Rajan with a salute. As he stepped out of the car, the S.P. took a good look around him.

The villagers who had gathered there seemed listless, subdued. The S.P. took in the sight of the canal and the nearby hill.

"So, Rudra, what other evidence have you dug up?"

"Nothing concrete yet, sir. But I am confident that we'll uncover something soon," Rudra replied, respectfully.

"Good. Now where is the local panchayat president?" asked the S.P. As he said it, his eyes went to Govinda Naicker, who was seated nearby crying.

"That's him, sir."

"I see. Where's that young fellow, the reporter?"

Rajendran—who had been standing to one side, watching everything around him keenly, like an X-ray scanner—stepped forward.

"Ah, there you are. Which magazine?"

"*Selvam*, sir."

"Isn't Raja Bhaskaran your editor?"

"Yes, sir."

"I was his senior…. We were in the same college."

"Oh!"

"What do you think of everything that's been happening around here?"

"What should I say, sir? However far science and technology progress, we still have these superstitious beliefs thriving, with talk of treasures and ritual sacrifices."

"Don't forget the superstitious people who put their money into chit funds and get scammed!"

"Quite right, sir."

"Okay… but I heard that you yourself claimed to have spoken to some spirits. Is it true?" Chidambara Rajan asked. Rajendran immediately looked to Rudra.

"Why are you looking at him?" said the S.P. "He's not going to believe any of it. But as for me, I think we should give everything a try."

"I'm glad to hear that, sir. Actually, in the beginning, I was as sceptical as Rudra sir. I didn't believe in any of it either. But after I experienced it myself… Now I'm a believer."

"Okay, so why don't you try summoning this spirit in front of me once? If the ghost can see who the murderer is and where he's hiding, that will help us a lot." Chidambara Rajan spoke casually, but it was clear to Rajendran that the S.P. was always thinking two steps ahead.

Next, Chidambara Rajan went straight to Naicker. Naicker's eyes were red with tears.

"Vanakkam, sir," Chidambara Rajan began politely. "I heard that the murdered man, Rajamanickam, was to have been your son-in-law."

"Yes sir. But it's not just him. Before Rajamanickam, there was another boy, Ganesan, who was supposed to have married my daughter. These sinners killed him, too. Not one, but two people have been murdered, and my daughter's life has been destroyed. I have never wished ill on anyone, not even an ant or a fly. Why is all this happening to me?"

"I understand your sorrow. But don't worry—it is our responsibility to capture those murderous dogs and bring peace to this village."

"You may be able to bring peace back to the village. But what about my poor daughter?" Naicker's question fell on Chidambara Rajan's chest like a heavy boulder.

"Be brave. It's not as though the wedding has taken place already. You will find another groom."

"Another groom? After all this, do you think anyone will willingly come forward?" Naicker rose as he posed this question.

Rajendran walked up to him boldly.

"Sir, don't worry. Your daughter will get married for sure. Go now, and make the necessary arrangements for Rajamanickam's funeral."

Rudra understood the meaning behind Rajendran's words. He gently patted Rajendran on the shoulder, as if congratulating him.

Naicker was not consoled by any of it. He began weeping loudly again. Chidambara Rajan stepped aside, as if giving him room to grieve, and began to walk away. Rudra and Rajendran followed him.

"Rudra—this canal bank and that hill—are these the two main locations?"

"Yes sir. We're searching both areas, inch by inch. And sub-inspectors Thanigaivel and Muthulingam are going from house to house in the village conducting a search as well."

"I doubt that anyone who is killing so brazenly would be hiding in the village. Moreover, that convict Irumbaadi knows exactly what the police are capable of. He must be hiding somewhere outside."

"Of course, sir. Our vigilance teams have gone to the neighbouring villages, too. We're expecting some information about the culprits any time now."

"Keep the police security in place until I say so. It will be good if we can set up a temporary office here in Aayakudi itself. Check with Naicker and see if there's an empty house we can use."

"There is, sir; I've already made the enquiries."

"Good. I hope you can maintain this efficiency." Chidambara Rajan gave another burst of instructions, and finally turned back to Rajendran.

"All right, thambi, we need to talk to the spirits now. How do you do it? Where do we need to go?"

"Sir, I'm staying with the village Tamil teacher, Deenadayalan. We can go to his house."

"Good. Then let's get going. Can we get there in the car?"

"No sir. But it's not very far away."

"Oh, if it's nearby, then fine. So, Rudra, are you going to come and watch us talk to the ghosts, or…?"

"No sir. I'm going to the crime scene. I'll leave it to you to plumb the depths of the spirit world." With this excuse, Rudra walked away.

Everyone who lived on Deenadayalan's street was standing outside and watching. They all wore forlorn expressions. The teacher, on seeing Chidambara Rajan approaching, stepped outside. As the S.P. stepped closer, he gave him a respectful welcome.

"So, you're the brave individual who first sent word to the magazine that there was a problem in this village?" said Chidambara Rajan. Rajendran realised that there was very little Chidambara Rajan didn't already know.

"Come inside, sir," said the teacher. "I don't know why it is, but we've had one tragedy after another. You have to help us put a stop to it."

"That's why I am here. Do you think your average police superintendent will come to try and talk to spirits? But here I am. Just wait and watch as the press and TV make fun of me tomorrow. 'Meet the S.P. who gets ghosts to help him catch criminals!'"

"But sir, every bit of information that Rajendran gathered while serving as a medium has turned out to be true! And it'll be the same this time, too. Just wait and see."

Rajendran left them to talk and stepped away to get ready. He washed his hands and feet, changed into a white veshti, came back in, and sat down. He had covered his forehead with ash.

The teacher brought the notebook and pen out.

"What's that for?" asked the S.P.

"This is what the ghost writes in, sir."

"Oh! Ghosts can write notes, can they?"

"That's one way they communicate. They've also entered the body of a young village girl and spoken through her."

"So the spirits use multiple platforms, eh?"

"Yes sir. Come, Rajendran thambi, please call Ramasamy now. Let the S.P. see," the teacher said, as he walked over to shut the front door. Rajendran closed his eyes and began to focus his mind on a single point.

The seconds began to dissolve.

A deep silence.

The pen in his hand was ready to start writing. Chidambara Rajan was watching it carefully.

But the pen refused to move.

The seconds stretched themselves out and became minutes. Deenadayalan looked slightly flustered and annoyed.

Eventually Rajendran gave up and opened his eyes.

"What happened, thambi?"

"I don't know what's wrong. Ramasamy's spirit is refusing to enter my body this time. He did tell us last time that the sorcerer was trying to catch hold of his spirit, and that it might be difficult for him to communicate with us. Maybe the sorcerer succeeded?"

Chidambara Rajan laughed loudly, in a tone that was plainly mocking.

Just then, a policeman arrived at the house. He was slightly overweight, with a small paunch, and he was panting—he'd been running.

He carried with him the news of the astrologer's death. The headless body had been found in a sugarcane field.

CHAPTER 19

DEENADAYALAN AND RAJENDRAN wore shocked expressions. Chidambara Rajan's gaze pierced through Rajendran as he heaved a sigh. The next moment, the S.P. was gone.

As the jeep came to a screeching halt in a cloud of dust near the sugarcane field, the policemen stood to attention. Chidambara Rajan jumped out of the vehicle and walked swiftly over to them. The sugarcane plants were tall, the leaves a light green colour. Small gusts of wind rustled through them across the field, like little children playing.

The astrologer's headless body lay in an irrigation ditch in the middle of the field. Blood must have spurted out like a fountain from his neck; plants up to ten feet away from the body were drenched in it. It was an extremely gory scene.

The man who had first spotted the corpse was being grilled by Rudra.

"Sir, I just came by to water the fields. I turned on the motor for the pump and the water came gushing through the channels. But I was shocked to see that the water was red! I ran along the ditch to see why and I found this headless body right here. I knew from his clothes that it was the josiyar; I had seen him just this morning on the road. I even asked him where he was going and he replied that Naicker Aiyya had sent for him. Now look at him… just lying here like this."

"Was there anyone else around when you found the body?"

"Not a soul, sir."

"Really?"

"I swear."

Rudra made him stand some distance away and returned to take a closer look at the body. It didn't look like the neck had been sliced during a fight, or with an angry stroke. It seemed to have been done neatly, as though someone had made the astrologer sit down and then carefully chopped his head off.

There were no footprints to be found, either.

As Rudra was examining the area, Chidambara Rajan reached his side.

Something seemed to weigh down heavily upon Rudra's head. He couldn't bring himself to look up and meet the S.P.'s eye.

"What ya… what is happening here?"

"I'm… I'm sorry, sir."

"What do you mean, sorry? You were over here, I was over there. In between us the whole village is crawling with policemen. And in the middle of all of it, another murder! The killer must think we're a bunch of inept fools!"

"I don't know what to say, sir. Whatever be the case, there will be no more unfortunate incidents here, sir."

"Enough, Rudra. You have twenty-four hours. I need to know who the murderer is by then!"

"Sir, I'm sure that it's Irumbaadi. I have no doubts about that. He has a sorcerer as an accomplice. These killings must all be linked to the treasure. See, the head alone is missing. Just like the bodies we found near the canal this morning."

"The reporters are already digging deep into this issue. Now this! They're going to rip us to shreds in the Legislative Assembly. We're going to hear from the Chief Minister soon, and he's going to tell me exactly the same thing I just told you. Twenty-four hours."

"Sir, I'll catch them. Irumbaadi and the sorcerer have to be hiding somewhere in the village."

"Then start looking for them!" Chidambara Rajan shouted.

By now, the teacher and Rajendran had arrived. They squirmed as they watched Rudra get a dressing down from Chidambara Rajan. When it was over, Rudra walked towards them. Rajendran tried to look him in the eye, but Rudra turned to the teacher.

"In the old stories, when people ask, *Who is greater, the protector or the crook?* they always answer, *The crook!* Looks like it's turning out to be true in real life as well!" lamented the teacher, in his scholarly fashion.

"Where can I find Naicker now?"

"He... I heard that he went to the hospital to see Rajamanickam's body."

"I need to see him now," said Rudra.

"If I meet him, I'll tell him," said the teacher, without much conviction.

"What Rajendran, why don't you ask your spirit where Irumbaadi and the sorcerer are hiding?" asked Rudra, mockingly.

Rajendran just laughed.

"You think it's a laughing matter, Rajendran?"

"No sir. I'm only laughing because I'm... puzzled."

"Leave all that. What did the spirit say?"

"It never came in the first place."

"What do you mean?"

"I'm sorry sir. My attempts today were unsuccessful."

"How can any attempt to call a non-existent spirit ever be successful?"

"Oh, let's not get into that argument again now. What are you going to do next?"

"I need to know what the astrologer and Naicker spoke about. I remember seeing him near the canal. Even then he looked sorrowful."

As he spoke, a jeep went past them and stopped in front of the houses. Four dogs leaped out, their trainers following behind, holding their leashes. The dogs were expert detection hounds from Kanyakumari, and they were ready to search each and every house. As a sub-inspector began making arrangements, they saw one of the dogs run up the street towards the teacher's house.

"By all means, let it go have a look," the teacher said.

"Something tells me those dogs won't be able to sniff out the killer," said Rajendran. He turned back to look again at the astrologer's body.

News of the latest murder was still spreading, and the crowd around the sugarcane field continued to grow. Among the newcomers was Thenmozhi, who stood behind another girl from the village, peeking at the headless corpse every now and then. She looked shaken.

Despite the large crowd that had gathered, the sorcerer was still hiding in the bushes some distance away, watching over everything. His eyes picked out Thenmozhi from the crowd.

"The virgin for the sacrifice has been found!" he whispered.

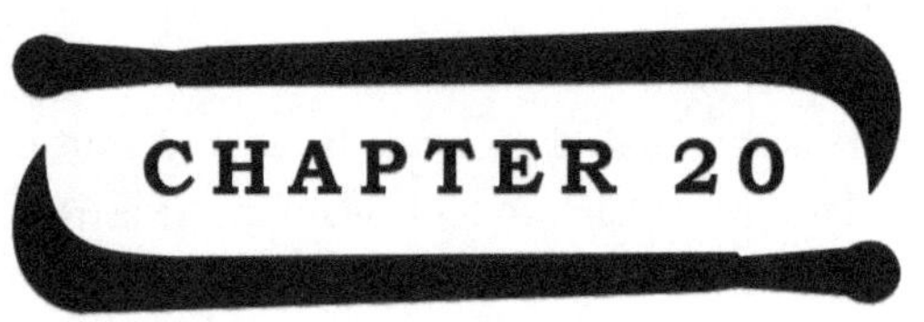

CHAPTER 20

THERE WERE TWO PATHS that led away from the sugarcane field into dense vegetation, but no one seemed to have noticed them. Even the sniffer dogs hadn't ventured in that direction.

Rudra's entire body was tensed. S.P. Chidambara Rajan, tired of standing around, started angrily walking back to his vehicle. He stopped halfway and turned back towards Rudra. Rudra quickly ran up to him.

"Rudra, when I say you have twenty-four hours, I mean exactly twenty-four hours. You have to apprehend both of them by then, both Irumbaadi and the sorcerer. I don't want to hear any excuses. Use however many bullets you need. Dead or alive, I don't care. But if you can't do it, you can hand in your resignation."

The anger in Chidambara Rajan's voice was boiling over. Even Thenmozhi heard it. She felt bad for Rudra.

Just then, a voice sounded out, "Hey! Thenu! What are you doing here?"

She turned.

It was Raangi, who worked in their house. She looked very worried.

"What is it, Raangi?"

"What are you doing here, pulla? Your mother's been looking for you everywhere."

"I heard that the astrologer had been killed. So I came here to see what had happened."

"You crazy child! The entire village is in a state of confusion. How could you come here by yourself without telling anyone?"

"I'll come back right away. Please don't tell my mother you saw me here. I'll just cut across the sugarcane field and walk along the irrigation canal to North Street and get home that way."

"No, no! You come with me. Your mother has given me strict instructions to make sure you get home at once."

"No, Raangi. If I come with you, she'll find out I was here. Just let me go—I'll be there in five minutes." As Raangi looked on helplessly, Thenmozhi hopped into the field and started making her way home.

Rajendran caught sight of her too and watched her run off, as gracefully as a leaping deer. Then he turned and walked towards Rudra, whose face was looking like a brinjal that had just been burnt in a fire.

"Sir..."

"Tell me, Rajendran."

"I have a theory. I don't think the source of this terror is human."

"What do you mean?"

"No normal human being, no matter how vicious a killer he might be, would be so bold as to keep on murdering one person after another with so many policemen crawling around the village. His instincts would be to lie low and protect himself."

"Then where do you think he is getting his courage from?"

"I think this is the work of someone with blind faith in the occult."

"There you go again with sorcery and magic! What a heap of dirt!"

"Don't dismiss the idea completely. Please consider that line of inquiry as well."

"Look Rajendran, this isn't the only village with ancient superstitions about treasures and human sacrifices. Ritualistic killings have been carried out in other places, too. But I've never heard of a real treasure being uncovered that way."

"Sir, I concede all of that. None of these murders is going to conjure a pile of gold here either. But the *belief* in the treasure must be what's driving the criminal to kill."

"Whatever his beliefs, he's not getting away with it!"

"He's already gotten away with two murders since you arrived."

"Listen, every one of my men has a photo of Irumbaadi with him. And the sorcerer will stand out in any crowd. It won't be hard to spot either of them."

"So you're convinced that it's Irumbaadi and the sorcerer, committing these crimes together?"

"I have no doubt about it. Naicker's wife Vanjiammal saw the sorcerer herself, just the other night!"

"Okay sir, but then shouldn't we be searching *outside* the village, too?"

Rudra laughed on hearing Rajendran's question. He pulled out his pistol, held it up, closed one eye and looked down the barrel.

"I get the feeling you're hiding something behind that laugh, sir."

"You *are* a journalist, aren't you? You catch on quick."

"I don't know what it is, though."

"In a case like this, a detective can't afford to look at things from just one perspective."

"I agree completely. You have to consider all the angles. But you still haven't answered my question."

"Rajendran, what if I told you that the killer was actually being protected? That right at this very moment, someone in the village is keeping him safe?"

Rudra's question made Rajendran's eyes widen. "Sir!"

"Don't ask me who that person is. All I'm saying is that there is someone. And all of this is his doing. I think he's seen the treasure, too."

Rajendran could only look astonished.

"There's a jeweller in Tirunelveli who recently got hold of about forty gold coins, each one weighing roughly ten grams. He'd been instructed to melt them down into biscuits. He noticed that some of the coins had

British-era symbols on them. He surreptitiously kept them, using some newer gold coins of his own to make the biscuits instead. He then sold the old coins to an antique collector for a good price. The collector was ready to buy as many coins as the jeweller could provide. This got the jeweller thinking. He started making coins himself and tried to pass them off as ancient specimens. But the collector soon realised that they were fakes and got furious. The issue escalated and ended up reaching the police.

"During that investigation, the police started looking into the man who'd brought the forty old coins to the jeweller in the first place. The jeweller didn't know his name, but he said he'd be able to identify him.

"We dug up pictures of all the known delinquents in the area, everyone who'd been arrested over the last few years. We put them all on slides and brought the jeweller to the station to look through them. Rajamanickam was one of the people in that set of photographs—and the jeweller identified him as the man who'd brought him the coins!"

At this point, Rudra was interrupted by a buzz from his wireless. He stepped to one side to listen.

Rajendran was stupefied. Until he'd met Rudra, he'd had quite a low opinion of the police; as far as he could figure, they weren't good for much besides catching bicyclists for trivial traffic violations. Now that whole perception had been turned on its head. Rudra loomed as large as a superhero in Rajendran's eyes.

He wrapped up his conversation over the wireless and returned. "So Rajendran, do you think I'm clutching at straws here?"

"No, I don't, sir. Please tell me everything. How many pages is this village's mystery going to fill?"

"Listen carefully. Around the same time that those coins turned up, Irumbaadi escaped from prison—with Rajamanickam's help—and started hiding out near that rocky hill. The two of them were preparing to hunt for the treasure together. It was then that this sorcerer, Marnad, showed up to assist them."

"You even know the sorcerer's name!?"

In response, Rudra just gave a quiet smile.

"Sir, when I watched you getting dressed down by the S.P., I thought you were stuck. But you seem to have made a lot of progress in this case!"

"What good has it done us? We still lost two more lives!"

"Could the two deaths have been prevented?"

"How could they have, when the criminals have someone else in Aayakudi helping them?"

"But your men went from door to door searching…?"

"Listen. A lot of this information, I haven't even shared with the S.P. yet. You're the only person I'm telling. As a journalist you might be able to shed some light on it."

"You have a lot of faith in me."

"Think long and hard, Rajendran. I'm sure something will pop up in your mind."

At these encouraging words from Rudra, sparks began to fly in Rajendran's brain.

* * *

Thenmozhi walked out of the sugarcane field past a little pond. She was just about to step onto North Street when a sharp thorn pierced her foot—*narukk!* She sat down on one side of the street and tried to pull the thorn out.

There was a large stack of fresh hay nearby. Something seemed to be digging itself out from the middle of it. In a moment, the sorcerer's head peered out from the hay, observing Thenmozhi. Then Marnad pushed the hay aside and walked towards her.

Only when he stood right next to her did Thenmozhi finally look up, startled. He looked into her eyes and fixed her with his mesmerizing stare. She didn't last longer than a few seconds before she succumbed.

"Follow me!" he said, and turned back towards the haystack. She walked behind him silently, without a word of protest. Marnad burrowed his way into the hay and then pulled Thenmozhi in after him.

There was not a soul around to see any of it.

The haystack closed up behind them.

CHAPTER 21

THE HOUSE WAS QUITE ORDINARY LOOKING. It had a roof made of rounded six-inch clay tiles. A bottle gourd creeper grew on the roof, unattended and withering. In the strong wind, the plant danced up and down like a snake.

The front of the house had a large granite-topped thinnai that could comfortably seat up to twenty people. Conveniently etched into the stone was a board to play *dayakattai*. Past the thinnai was a big hall. Next was a grain cupboard, and then a number of rooms with large doors fitted with iron handles. There was an MGR calendar stuck to the wall. Spiderwebs formed cradles here and there, with spiders the size of tamarind seeds perched inside.

Singaram, one of Naicker's farm labourers, had just opened the house up for Rudra and was showing him around. Rajendran was with them as well.

"It's nice," said Rudra. "Is there a toilet at the back?"

"Toilet? You mean the *kakoos*?"

"That's right."

"Yes. There's a well back there too. You'll need to draw whatever water you need from there. There's a tank next to the well; if you fill it up, it should hold enough for about fifty people."

"Good. We'll use this house for now. Please let Naicker know."

"So this is the Aayakudi police post from now on?" asked Rajendran.

"That's right. We need to house thirty or forty policemen, and it has to be somewhere right in the village. They all need to be able to bathe and change their clothes and everything."

"Perhaps this could even become a permanent setup?"

"That's not in my hands. By the by, do you remember what you said earlier, about you going your way and me going mine?"

"Yes, I do. Why do you bring it up?"

"Two hours have passed since the S.P. gave me my deadline. I have to capture the criminals within the next twenty-two hours, and make sure nobody else gets killed in the meantime."

"I understand sir. You're asking me to follow my own path. Two heads are better than one when it comes to hunting for these criminals. That what you're getting at, isn't it?"

"Yes. Follow your instincts. In case of emergency, if you need to contact me, use my secret cell phone number. Make a note of it."

Rajendran took down the number.

"All the best, Rajendran!"

"Best to you too, sir."

They shook hands, and Rajendran opened the front door.

He stepped out to find a woman standing at the doorstep with a child in her arms. She looked to be in a very pitiful condition; sorrow was spread thick across her face. Rajendran stopped in front of her. Rudra saw her too, and came up to meet her.

"Vanakkam sir," she said.

"What's the matter, amma?"

"I'm a native of this village. My husband is a mason. He was building a house near Courtallam."

"Why are you telling us this?"

"Well, my neighbours told me that we have a police station in our own village now, and that if I wanted to file a complaint, I should come here."

"What's the complaint?"

"My husband's been missing for the past ten days. His name is Bangaru. I've been under the impression that he was in Courtallam all this while. But today someone from Courtallam came here looking for him!" As the words came out of her mouth, tears began pouring from her eyes.

Rudra's face showed worry lines. "How do you know your husband hasn't gone somewhere else?"

"He has nowhere else to go! Both of our families live right here in Aayakudi."

"Has he ever done anything like this before?"

"Oh, he might be able to stay away from me, but he simply cannot bear to be without his child. She's his life. He's never been apart from us for this long before."

"I'll need a written complaint. Put down all of this information, along with his name and other identification marks, and give it to me. I'll pass it on to the station in charge of this area. They'll take action."

"This isn't really a police station, then?"

"Not a permanent one, no. We're just staying here temporarily. Someone's given you wrong information."

"I can't read or write sir. But I have a photograph from our wedding I can give you." She pulled a picture from the folds of her sari. "Maybe you can use this…"

The two newlyweds stood smiling, decked in garlands. Bangaru was wearing a half-sleeved silk shirt. On the exposed parts of his arms were large black marks.

"What are those?" asked Rudra, pointing at his arms.

"Oh, he's had those marks from the time he was born, sir."

Rudra looked like a jolt of electricity had just run through him. Rajendran watched as his body tensed up and his brow furrowed.

Then he grabbed the photo, ran towards a jeep that was parked nearby, and jumped in.

"Kalimuthu! Drive straight to the mortuary!" Rajendran heard him say.

"Sir, what's going on? Where's the inspector taking the photograph?" the woman asked Rajendran.

"Please be patient. He'll come back soon and explain everything," he answered her, and began walking towards the teacher's house.

* * *

Raangi returned home. Her eyes hunted around the house for Thenmozhi, who was supposed to have taken the shortcut.

Vanjiammal saw her. "What, di, where's Thenu?" she asked, walking out of the kitchen.

"H-hasn't she retuned yet, aatha?" Raangi stammered.

"You're answering me with the same question I'm asking you! Didn't I tell you to go bring her back home?"

"I did find her, aatha, and I asked her to come home with me. But instead she told me to go home and she ran into the sugarcane field."

"Why did you let her leave? Don't you know the state the village is in?"

"But aatha…."

"Don't you 'but aatha' me! How could you let this happen? The one person who *really* should be sitting inside the house right now is out there gallivanting around!"

Naicker was sitting outside with some relatives who had come to offer their condolences for Rajamanickam's death. When Vanjiammal's loud cries reached his ears, he gave a pained look.

He got up, went inside and asked, "Hey pulla, why are you shouting so much?"

"You know that stupid little curry leaf whose birth you prayed so hard for? Well she isn't here. She went to see what all the fuss was about with the astrologer's body in the sugarcane field. What, should I just sit around like it doesn't bother me?" Vanjiammal's questions pierced Naicker like arrows.

"But why do you have to shout so loudly that people can hear you from four streets away? How about when she returns, you just break her leg and lock her up in a room."

"Oh, don't worry about that, I'll break a lot more than just one leg. When are the police going to give us Rajamanickam's body?"

"What are we supposed to do with a headless corpse? They've put the body in a freezer in the big hospital. Not one, but four bodies lined up. None of them have heads!"

"So, until they find the head, we can't perform any of the last rites?"

"I don't think so. Nothing we can do but wait," muttered a resigned Naicker as he walked back outside.

Vanjiammal turned to Raangi. "Hey! You go right now. Find out where Thenmozhi is—and don't come back without her. Otherwise I don't ever want to see your face again. *Go!*"

A determined look came over Raangi's face.

As she walked out of the house, she overheard one of the mourners say, "What are those crooks planning to do with his head? It's all so mysterious!"

None of them knew that Thenmozhi was now in line to be sacrificed as well.

* * *

The teacher's house.

Rajendran was drawing water from the well in the back and taking a bath. There was a renewed energy about him. The teacher noticed it too.

"A bath, at this hour? How come, thambi?"

He picked up a towel to dry his hair and replied, "Vaadhyare, I am going to talk to the spirits again!"

"I thought they didn't turn up the last time."

"Last time, I called Ramasamy and Ganesan's spirits. Maybe the sorcerer had already taken hold of them by then. This time, though, I'm not planning on calling either of those two."

"Then who are you going to call?"

"The astrologer. He's the last one to have been killed."

"The astrologer? But will he come?"

"I'm going to try and see! Rudrapathy is proceeding at high speed in one direction. I'm doing what I can to help."

"High speed, eh? *Podalanga!* People are still dying."

"I understand your frustration sir. But don't make the same mistake I did and underestimate the police. Rudra is not your average policeman. He's uncovered a lot of information!"

"What has he found out?"

"You'll be amazed when you hear. Let me tell you this: All the murders are linked to the treasure. Irumbaadi, along with the sorcerer Marnad, are the ones responsible. But someone else in the village has been helping them, too."

"What are you saying, thambi?"

"First, let me contact the astrologer's spirit and see if he can tell us anything more. We can discuss the rest later. Rudra has rushed off to the mortuary, carrying a photograph of a man from your village—Bangaru."

"Bangaru, the mason?"

"I think so."

"What happened to him?"

"Apparently he's been missing for the past ten days. His wife came crying to the police with his photograph."

As he said this, Rajendran's cell phone rang. He pulled it out of his pocket and looked at the screen. It was Rudra.

"Sir?"

"Rajendran, some bad news."

"What is it, sir?"

"The body with the disfigured face—the one we thought was Irumbaadi's at first. It's the body of Bangaru, that woman's husband."

"Sir!!"

"I'm here at the mortuary. All the identification marks in the wedding photograph match with the body here."

"So that means the first murder was Bangaru. Next was Ramasamy. Third was Ganesan. Fourth was Rajamanickam. And the astrologer was the fifth. Am I right?"

"Exactly! Except that Ramasamy's head wasn't cut off. Neither was Bangaru's—just his face was mangled. It's only after the first two that the headless corpses started appearing."

"What are you getting at, sir?"

"I think the treasure has already been found. But there were a lot of people involved, and now they're all getting killed off one after another."

"How did you come up with this theory?"

"Just a hunch. I think they started cutting off and hiding the heads just to confuse the police."

"Sir, come back to the village soon. I'm on my way down my own path, to see if I can confirm your hunch."

Rajendran put the phone down and quickly began preparing himself. Again, he took some sacred ash and applied it to his forehead. He spread out a towel, lit a few sticks of incense, and picked up the notebook and pen. He sat down and slowly pushed away all of the numerous thoughts in his head. He tried to focus only on the astrologer.

The teacher sat there watching him.

Rajendran's mind called out, *Hey josiyare! Come here! Come and help us make sense of all this!*

This time, his efforts did not go to waste. The astrologer's spirit possessed him, and Rajendran's pen began to move.

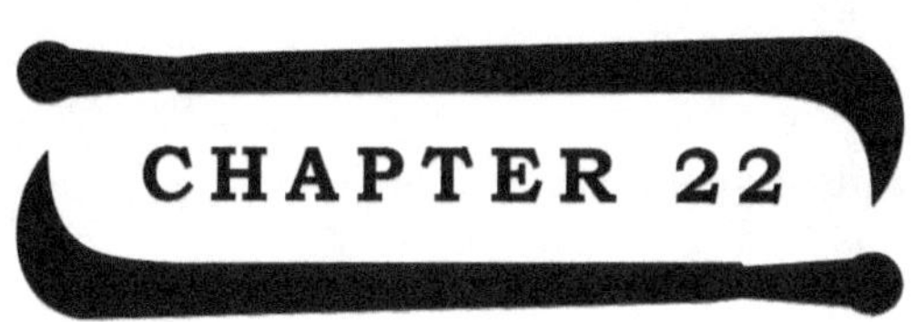

CHAPTER 22

"Many thanks for calling me, thambi! Ask whatever you want, and I will answer."

With that, the writing stopped and Rajendran sat still, like a statue.

"Rajendran…? Thambi…? The josiyar's spirit is here," said the teacher. "It's asking you if you have any questions. Come on, this is a good opportunity. Get all of your doubts clarified."

Immediately, the pen began to move over the notebook.

Who is that?

On reading the question, the teacher quickly responded.

"It is me, josiyare, Deenadayalan. The Tamil teacher."

Rajendran's hand ran across the paper once more. Another question.

Ah vaadhyar ! Why did you call me?

"Josiyare, who killed you? What's going on here in Aayakudi?"

Ask the questions one by one.

"All right. Who killed you?"

The sorcerer Marnad.

"Why did he do it?"

So that he could get hold of the treasure.

"Has the treasure already been found?"

Yes. It's here in the village.

"Who were his accomplices?"

That's a big secret. I don't know.

"Can't you find out? Don't you spirits have any special powers?"

I'll only gain those powers once my family performs my last rites and makes the necessary offerings. Hand my body over to my son and ask him to conduct my funeral.

"I'll tell them to do so. Where is this Marnad hiding now?"

I can see that he is inside a large haystack. But I can't tell where it is.

"Why is it so difficult for even you to find him?"

He's a very skilful sorcerer. He can take control of practically anything—dogs, cats, birds and even snakes. He could be sitting right next to you, and you would be unaware of his presence.

"How do we catch him then?"

I don't know myself. That is why I am roaming.

"So, what *do* you know then?"

I know that there are sure to be more murders. No one can stop them. Once he cuts off eight heads to offer to the eight directions, he will complete the spell with the ninth and final sacrifice. Then he will take full control of all directions. Only then can he leave Aayakudi with the loot. Otherwise he will never be able to fight his way past the Goddess Jakkamma, who guards the treasure.

"You know all of that, and yet you still can't tell us where the treasure is hidden?"

The only reason I know as much as I do is that Marnad told me before he cut my head off. I was a sacrifice to Jakkamma myself!

"The police will really make mincemeat of him when they catch him."

He can foresee his own future. He knows many spells. Only someone who is blessed by the spirits can even approach him. No one else can touch him.

"How is this helpful, josiyare? On one hand the police are looking everywhere for him. On the other, there is a death every day."

It is nothing but fate. The result of our sins. I paid the price for mine. My greed drove me to make false predictions, and this is the result.

"Didn't you know when your own end was going to come?"

I was a worthless astrologer. My predictions hardly ever come true for anyone else, and I couldn't foresee my own fate either. I assisted thugs like Rajamanickam. And I met my end, just the same as he did.

"Okay, but where is the treasure now? Where is Marnad? And who's helping him from here in our village? When will you be able to answer these three questions?"

I don't know. I only know one thing for sure—he's hiding inside a haystack. He went there after killing me, carrying my head with him. From the outside, it looks like a normal haystack. But inside is where he performs all his sacrifices. He has an image of Jakkamma there; he placed my head in front of it and did some rituals. Then he took my head and buried it in the southwest corner of the village. He planted some black and red ebony bushes on top so that the dogs won't dig it up. He also applied a dark ink to the plant and chanted the Bairava mantra one hundred times. Afterwards, he pulled out one of the plant's roots, made a ring out of it, and put it on his finger. As long as he has that ring on, no dogs can get near him or his hiding place. If they do come close, they'll just suddenly lie down and curl up.

"Okay. I think you've given us enough for now. We'll reach out to you again when we have the police with us. You must make another appearance then, and answer whatever questions we have."

A warning! Make sure this conversation remains a secret. Otherwise it won't be difficult for Marnad to capture my spirit as well.

"Thank you for your warning, and for everything you've told us. You may go now."

Rajendran regained his senses immediately. On his lap was the notebook with all the information that the astrologer's ghost had provided.

"Thambi, see how much the josiyar has told us! I asked the questions myself this time."

Rajendran read the notes eagerly. But only two bits of information seemed to be of much use. One was the confirmation of Rudra's hunch that the treasure had already been found. The other was the news that the sorcerer was hiding inside a haystack.

Rajendran didn't waste any time. He called Rudra on his cell phone at once.

"Rudra sir."

"Yes, Rajendran?"

"You were right. The treasure's been found."

"Did your spirits tell you?"

"Yes. Marnad is the killer. He's still in the village. He's hiding inside a haystack."

"A haystack?"

"Yes. Also, the heads of the murder victims have already been buried in various corners of the village. There are bushes planted on top of them to prevent your dogs from sniffing them out."

"What are you saying, Rajendran? The police have been patrolling the village day and night. How can he be strolling around burying heads? That ghost of yours doesn't seem to be making any sense."

"Sir, Marnad is well-versed in magic. The josiyar says he can walk right past a person without being seen. Also, he might not have done the actual burying himself. Any of his accomplices could have done it for him."

"Did the ghost tell you who the accomplices are?"

"He says he doesn't know."

"Then you haven't found out anything of value at all! Just tall tales about haystacks and heads!"

"But sir, can't you arrange to have all of the haystacks searched? What's the harm in trying?"

"Yes, yes, I'll get that done. Also, you said he'd planted bushes on top of the heads. Do you know what kind?"

"The spirit said they were red and black ebony, sir."

"Do plants like that even exist? Anyway, I'll have my men look for them."

"It's simple sir. He says that dogs will lie down and curl up the moment they go near these bushes."

"Hmm. All right, Rajendran. Is that everything you've managed to find out?"

"For now, sir."

"Then let me give you something bigger than what your ghost gave you."

"What's that, sir?"

"Your dear Thenmozhi, Naicker's daughter. We saw her go into the sugarcane field, remember?"

"Yes."

"Well, now she's missing. Naicker was just here wailing about it, saying that he suspects that the sorcerer has kidnapped her. He's filed a complaint."

"*Sir!*"

"Looks like your ghosts don't tell you the important things." Grim sarcasm dripped from Rudra's voice.

Rajendran was crushed. He took a long time to recover from the blow. Slowly, he got up, and started looking for the teacher. But Deenadayalan didn't seem to be anywhere inside the house.

Where had he gone?

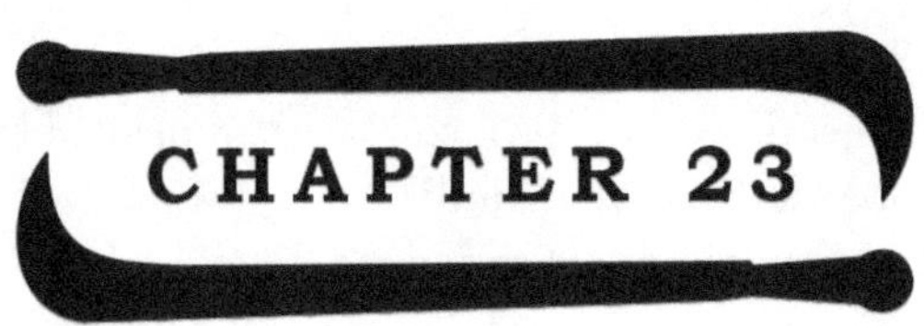

CHAPTER 23

RAJENDRAN WAS SCARED. Where had the teacher disappeared to?

He called out to him loudly as he circled the house. Then he saw him walking through some bushes in the back yard and heaved a sigh of relief.

"What, thambi? Did you think I was missing? Did I send you into a panic?" he asked as he washed his feet.

"You did shake me up there for a minute!"

"I thought I heard you on the phone with Rudrapathy."

"Yes. Naicker has received another blow. In a way, I did as well."

"What, thambi?"

"Thenmozhi has gone missing."

"What? Really?!"

"Yes. And now I don't know what to do."

"How terrible! Such unimaginable things are happening!"

"This is no time for more talk. I'm making a move."

"Where to?"

"I'm going to look in every single haystack around the village. The police must have started their search already—I'm going to join them." Rajendran jumped to his feet and left.

Up until now, everything that had happened in Aayakudi had affected Rajendran's mind alone. But Thenmozhi's disappearance had deeply impacted his heart. That much was perfectly clear to the teacher from the younger man's wilted expression.

The teacher wondered to himself whether Rajendran had fallen in love.

* * *

Rudra had cleverly planned his next steps. There was a water tank in the middle of the village which had once supplied water to all of Aayakudi, but it had stopped functioning many years ago. Today, it came in very handy for Rudra.

He climbed on top of it and surveyed the entire village through his binoculars. He could see every house clearly.

To an observer below, it appeared as though he was looking around at random. But in fact, his sights were focused only on those houses that had large haystacks. Keeping the setting sun as his reference, he marked out the northeast, northwest, southeast and southwest corners of the village.

Without moving from his place, he pulled out his wireless and began instructing his team.

"Shanmugam, there are a total of twenty haystacks in the village. Only two of them are located at any distance from the houses. Those two also look bigger than the others. It's likely that Marnad is hiding inside one of them. Get two groups to take their weapons and surround both of those haystacks at once. One of them is over by the pond. The other is in the field behind the bus stop."

As soon as he heard Rudra's instructions, S.I. Shanmugam began working at lightning speed. He assembled two rows of ten armed policemen each. They stood strong and at attention, motionless as Shanmugam walked around them. He spoke briefly; then they all saluted him in unison and quickly dispersed.

The entire village watched in stunned silence. Chinna Pechi was there in the crowd as well. Once again, her eyes held that familiar angry glare!

Rajendran had reached the water tower. He craned his neck to look up at Rudra, and then followed the inspector's gaze towards the group of policemen approaching the haystack by the pond.

Suddenly his cell phone called out as if to say, *Talk to me.* Irritated, he gave it his ear.

On the other end was his editor. "What, ya? Have you settled down in that village for good? Can't even make a single phone call?" he started off agitatedly.

"I'll call you back soon sir. We're about to get to the bottom of this whole mess. We'll talk after some time," Rajendran said curtly, as he broke into a run.

The haystack was surrounded by policemen, each of them standing an equal distance from the next.

S.I. Shanmugam began digging into the hay, holding his revolver ready in the other hand. Just as he expected, the hay was only two feet deep. Behind it was a wooden plank which served as a door; when he pulled it away, a sort of hollowed-out cave was revealed within.

Inside, Thenmozhi lay unconscious, a rag stuffed into her mouth. Her hands were tied behind her back.

Rajendran, peering over Shanmugam's shoulder, breathed a sigh of relief.

Around her was a jumble of articles: billhooks, goat heads, pots and pans, a large number of eggs, some dolls made out of dough, and many other strange items. Thenmozhi lay in the middle of all of it, curled up like a question mark.

The sorcerer, though, was missing.

Rajendran pushed past Shanmugam and began untying the ropes around Thenmozhi's hands. Then he carried her out, still unconscious, the hay brushing against their faces.

By this time the village folk had gathered around the haystack. Naicker and his wife had arrived as well. They approached, hesitantly. Rajendran lay Thenmozhi down in front of them at the edge of the pond. He quickly scooped up some water in his palms and sprinkled it over Thenmozhi's face.

S.I. Shanmugam was carefully gathering all the items that were inside the structure. When he brought out a billhook with a handkerchief wrapped around its handle, Naicker's eyebrows arched.

Rajendran, however, was focused on Thenmozhi alone. He didn't acknowledge any of the others who were standing around. When she came to and saw him up close, her eyelids fluttered.

Despite all the commotion, Rudra did not come down from the water tank. He stayed in place, his eyes circling the entire village like a hawk. Scanning the area with his binoculars, he spotted two people trying to make a quick getaway.

As he adjusted the focus, he realised that they'd been very smart. Right now, everyone in Aayakudi was gathered by the pond. Half of the policemen were still searching near the bus stop. The criminals had taken advantage of the distraction to make their escape.

But Rudra was not going to allow it. He took hold of the long rifle that was hanging from his shoulder. It had a small sniper scope affixed to the top, the diameter of a one-rupee coin. In the middle of the scope was a small plus sign. He moved the rifle slowly until the plus sign was directly over the back of one of the people running.

He pulled the trigger.

Without a sound, the bullet gained freedom, flew through the air, smashed through the first man's backbone and settled in his chest. He crumpled. His partner redoubled his speed, but the next moment, a second bullet went through his back as well.

Both of them fell, like banana trees chopped at the base of the stem.

Thenmozhi opened her eyes and stood up. Vanjiammal hugged her tightly and began crying. Rajendran felt a great sense of relief.

In the second haystack, the police discovered another hiding spot. Irumbaadi's clothes, his leather bag, and his gun were found inside, along with a pot containing a strange ink-like substance. The police collected all of it as evidence.

Rudra looked at his wristwatch as he climbed down from the tower. It had been eight hours since his discussion with S.P. Chidambara Rajan. Both of the criminals had been shot down, and the missing Thenmozhi had been found as well.

The thought gave him comfort.

S.I. Shanmugam, Rajendran and Thenmozhi were all headed towards him. Rajendran's face was flooded with joy. The ghost had been proved correct, and even more importantly, Thenmozhi was safe and sound!

Shanmugam approached Rudra and saluted him.

"Listen, Shanmugam… Irumbaadi and Marnad are lying dead on the path leading out of the village. Go and secure the bodies right away," Rudra instructed.

Rajendran gaped in amazement. "Sir, how?" he asked.

In response, Rudra raised his rifle and took aim at a point in the distance.

Rajendran understood. "Oh, so that's why you stayed on top of the water tank? But we never heard the shot!"

"This rifle has a silencer, Rajendran."

Thenmozhi stood between her parents, hanging her head. Naicker approached Rudra, his palms together.

"Sir, you've managed to rescue my daughter and save the village as well," he said.

"Only with the help of this journalist right here," he said, pointing at Rajendran.

Rajendran responded excitedly, "Sir! So now do you believe in ghosts?"

"Why don't you ask them to come and talk to me directly?" Rudra's words were loaded with kilograms of sarcasm.

"But you've already caught the killers! What else do you need from the ghosts?"

"What do you mean, what else do I need? We still need to find the other criminal—the one who's been assisting the two killers from within the village this whole time!"

Rajendran didn't know what to say.

"Besides, aren't you even a little interested to know what's become of that multi-crore ancient treasure?"

Rudra's police brain continued to blaze, embers flying.

Two stretchers carrying Irumbaadi and Marnad's bodies reached them. Thenmozhi shivered as she caught sight of the sorcerer's body. She hugged Vanjiammal tightly.

One by one, the heads that had been buried under the bushes around the village were retrieved as well.

All the while, Chinna Pechi stood to one side, watching.

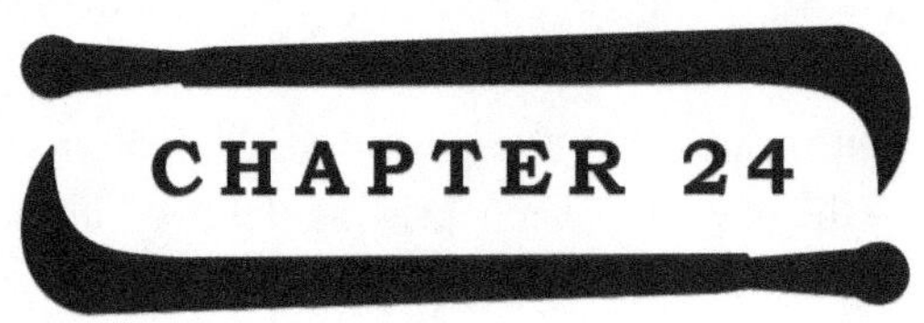

CHAPTER 24

No one in the crowd took notice of Chinna Pechi except Rudra, whose policeman's eyes kept looking over to check on her from time to time.

At that point the teacher showed up, looking as if he was just returning from some errand. As he walked into the street, he found Marnad and Irumbaadi's bodies on one side of him and the recovered heads lined up on the other. He shivered at the grisly scene, then pulled himself together.

"Rudrapathy! You have somehow managed to succeed!" he said as he stuck out his right hand and shook Rudra's.

Rudra looked pleased at the praise. A compliment from one's former teacher is always something special.

"It's not over yet, aiyya," said Rajendran, turning the teacher's attention his way. "Rudra sir says that the most important criminal is yet to be caught."

The teacher reacted to this as though he'd been hit in the middle of his forehead with a hammer. He quickly turned to look back at Rudra, but the policeman had stepped away to give S.I. Shanmugam some instructions.

"What are you saying, thambi?" he asked, turning back to Rajendran. "Are we still not free from the demons that torment our village?"

"No sir. These two, Irumbaadi and Marnad, were comfortably hiding inside a couple of haystacks right here in the village while they committed all of these murders. And someone else has been helping them right from the start. That person still needs to be found." Rajendran paused. "There's also the question of where the treasure is. That's what was behind all the killing. So, the most important thing now is to find it, don't you think?"

"Certainly, certainly," mumbled the teacher. "As the saying goes: even after the rain stops, the drizzle continues."

Rudra returned.

"Rudrapathy… Rajendran thambi just told me a few things. It looks like your work here is not yet done."

"That's right, sir," said Rudra. "It would have helped if these two had been caught alive; we could have found out who their accomplice was, and where he was hiding the treasure. But I was forced to shoot them."

"You've come this far. I'm sure you'll be able to find the last man as well," the teacher said confidently.

Now Naicker approached them. He walked up to Rudra and quietly held both his hands. His eyes were moist.

"What is it, Naicker? Why are you still tearing up?"

"I can't help it. You may have put an end to the murders— but what is to become of my daughter?"

"Don't worry about her. I'm sure you'll find her a suitable groom."

"Remember, this isn't the big city! You can't hide anything from anyone here in the village. My daughter's bad luck has swallowed the lives of not one but two grooms, one after the other. Who do you think will come forward to marry her, knowing that?" he wailed sorrowfully. At his side, Thenmozhi hung her head low, and Vanjiammal sighed heavily.

Rudra turned towards Rajendran and gave him a look. Rajendran understood, and silently signalled his assent.

"Naicker! Would you have any objections if *I* found a groom for your daughter?"

Naicker looked taken aback. "You? Where are *you* going to find a groom?"

"I've already found him. He's a good lad, with a well-paying job. If you're okay with it, I can ask him to tie a thaali around your daughter's neck right here and now!"

The suddenness of this announcement made everyone's heads turn.

A look of joy had come over Deenadayalan's face. "Naicker, I think I know who Rudrapathy means. Your daughter is very fortunate. I do hope you'll agree to it."

"How can I agree when you won't even tell me who you're talking about?"

"It's none other than our journalist, Rajendran!" Rudra pointed at Rajendran, who gave Naicker a slightly nervous smile.

A look of shock came over Naicker's face. Then it slowly changed to worry.

"Naicker!" the teacher interjected. "What are you waiting for? I've gotten to know Rajendran thambi quite well. He is a gem of a boy. And I think your daughter likes him too. Love blossomed between the two of them a while ago, but thambi has kept it under wraps."

Naicker turned to his daughter questioningly.

Her answer was clear in her eyes.

Vanjiammal went up to her husband swiftly. "Say yes. What more do you need to think about now?"

"There's nothing more to fear, Naicker," said Rudra. Not even a petty crime will take place in this village henceforth. We've pulled the evil up by the roots. Say yes. Let all this bitterness come to an end in the sweet celebration of a wedding!"

Naicker finally nodded in agreement. Thenmozhi hugged her mother tightly in joy.

"There are only six more days to go before Jupiter loses its power according to her horoscope," Naicker said. "I would like to have the wedding ceremony before that. Do you have any objections?"

Rajendran assured him that he did not.

* * *

Egmore Station, Chennai.

As Rajendran got down from his compartment, his editor Raja Bhaskar was waiting for him.

"Sir, you?!" Rajendran was astonished.

"Yes, it's me. How was your journey, Rajendran?"

"Everything was good, sir. But what is this! You've come all the way to the station yourself? I'm feeling a little awkward!"

"Ada... It's the least I could do. You've achieved something great as a journalist. It was the clues you gathered that helped crack the case! That's hardly a small matter. I felt I had to come and congratulate you in person."

They walked towards the car park. Raja Bhaskar picked up Rajendran's luggage himself and put it in the dickey. Then he got into the driver's seat.

Rajendran, delighted by the affectionate welcome, got in next to him. The car started.

"You've carried out the responsibilities I entrusted to you very well. Inspector Rudra spoke to me for a long time over the telephone. You've been a great support to him."

"Not really, sir. He's very smart and capable on his own."

"I'm told that you still haven't gotten quite to the bottom of it though—the main reason for the killings."

"Yes sir. We still don't know where the treasure is. Nor do we know the identity of the person who was helping the murderers."

"Couldn't that ghost answer those questions for you?" asked Raja Bhaskar, needling him.

"No sir. It didn't know."

"That's what I find confusing. These spirits of yours seem to be quite ignorant!"

Rajendran didn't know what to say.

"Don't take this the wrong way Rajendran. But think about it. Humans have limits on this earth. Does it make any sense to you for spirits to have limited knowledge as well?"

"Sir, what are you getting at?"

"I want you to write up all your experiences as a series of articles in the magazine. But I think you need proper clarity on this point before you start."

With that, the car turned into the parking lot of Hotel Dasaprakash.

"Come on. Let's have some tiffin and a nice degree coffee."

"Sir, my mother must be waiting eagerly to see me at home."

"Don't worry. I've already told her that I'd drop you home myself."

"Oh! So you planned all this well ahead."

"I have a lot of things to discuss with you. You'll be returning to Aayakudi tonight itself. Then the day after tomorrow is your wedding! And after that you'll be off on your honeymoon vacation for ten or fifteen days. So this is our only chance to talk things over."

"Sir, I'm sorry I didn't have a chance to tell you about my wedding myself. Please don't take it the wrong way."

"What's there to misunderstand? I'm quite happy for you; you've found the right girl at the right time. I look at you as a true journalist. You have all the right qualities: courage, enterprise, sacrifice, everything. There's only one thing that I can't come to terms with, and that's the fact that you believe in ghosts! You even say you spoke to them!"

By the time Raja Bhaskar reached the topic of spirits, they were seated inside the AC dining hall. Raja Bhaskar wiped his glasses.

"Sir, neither Rudra nor I believed in any of it at the beginning," said Rajendran. "But I had so many experiences, one after the other… it was only because of a clue the spirits gave me that we were able to find the criminals' hiding place inside the haystack. That was the information that finally helped us crack the case!"

"Yes. And that's exactly how Rudra identified the real culprit, too!"

Rajendran grabbed the table with both hands. He sat bolt upright. "What?"

"I haven't said anything yet. I'm not sure you'll believe me when I do."

"Why are you dragging this out sir? Tell me what you mean."

"Don't worry, I'll tell you. That's exactly why I brought you here." Raja Bhaskar gestured to the waiter. He ordered coffees and two poori sets. Then he rubbed his hands together lightly, and began.

"What time did you leave Aayakudi yesterday?"

"At about four in the afternoon."

"What would you say if I told you that by five o'clock, Rudra had arrested the teacher, Deenadayalan?"

The news fell on Rajendran like a sledgehammer.

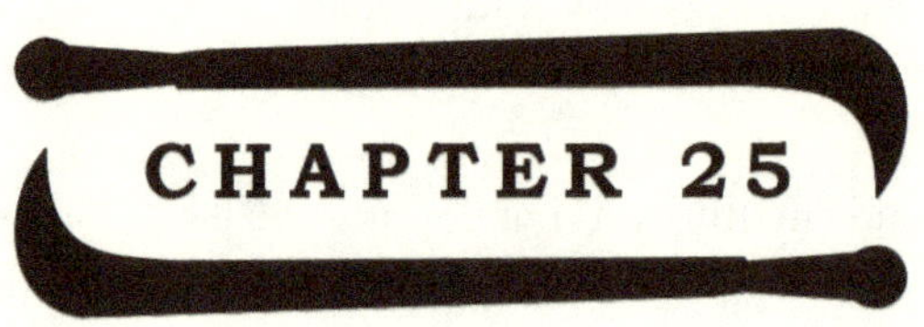

CHAPTER 25

IT WAS AS IF THE SKY ITSELF had crumbled and fallen on Rajendran's head. He looked back at Raja Bhaskar in disbelief.

"What, Rajendran? Shocked?"

"Yes, sir, I am! On what basis did Rudra come to suspect him?"

"They say that a reporter is half a policeman. But it saddens me to hear you ask such a question. It makes me think that you're barely a quarter of a policeman!"

"Sir, please! I'm not interested in becoming half a policeman, or even a quarter of one. I'm happy to remain a reporter. But please tell me what happened! The teacher was the one who wrote to us in the first place. He's the one who shined a light on all the problems facing the village. He gave me a place to stay in his own home, and fed me as well. He helped me in every way possible." Rajendran was becoming emotional, gripping the table even harder.

"Don't get worked up. I won't deny that he did all of that. But that's just one side of the man. He has another side to him, and it's a nasty one."

"How did you find out about all of this?"

"Don't be angry Rajendran. Why are you getting hysterical? It's good to get deeply involved in an issue, but it looks like you're overly invested here. That's dangerous."

"Sir, please tell me. On what basis did Rudra suspect the teacher and arrest him?"

"It's true that Deenadayalan wrote that letter to us. But he didn't sign his name, did he?"

"That's right—he wrote it under Chinna Pechi's name. But he explained his reasons for doing so."

"Oh, he might have given a thousand explanations. But that's where he did something stupid while trying to act smart. Rudra began to suspect him right then."

"Sir, Rudra was Deenadayalan's student! How could he suspect his own guru?"

"That's the way a policeman's mind works. He might be looking at you and saying one thing while doing the exact opposite behind your back. If the teacher was an honest man, as you say, then he should have gone to the police in the first place. Only after he'd tried that and gotten nowhere should he have reached out to democracy's fourth pillar, the press."

"Sir, are you really saying that the teacher was the root cause of all of the problems in Aayakudi?"

"Not *the* root cause, but one of them. Listen carefully. When he wrote to us, Deenadayalan had decided on two possible plans of action. One if we disregarded the letter and threw it away, the other if we gave it credence and acted on it."

"So, what would he have done if you hadn't sent me there?"

"Even then, there would have been a series of murders in the village. He wanted to make sure that he didn't go to the police till the very end. If by chance the police got there and arrested him, then the letter was to be one of his alibis. Essentially, he could claim that he wrote to the press about the problems in the village, but no one paid heed. He thought that he could use that as an excuse to escape suspicion."

"But why should he use Pechi's name to write the letter? He could have used his own name instead!"

"That's exactly what confirms that he has a criminal mind. Pechi's father Ramasamy was one of the people who was killed. Deenadayalan wanted to create an opportunity where he could say that he believed that the action would be swift if the letter came from an affected party, like Ramasamy's daughter."

"Sir, I am very confused."

"Okay, I'll try to explain. Originally there were three people who knew about the treasure in the Aayakudi rocks: Deenadayalan, Irumbaadi, and a third accomplice, whose identity we still don't know. They joined hands to dig it up. But while they were in the process of retrieving it, they were spotted by a fourth person—Ramasamy, Chinna Pechi's father. They had no choice but to bring him into the group. Working together, the four of them dug up the treasure.

"Only then did the problems begin. There is still a strong belief in rural areas that anyone who digs up an ancient treasure will be attacked by ghosts. Neither the teacher, nor Irumbaadi, nor the third man thought much of that superstition; but Ramasamy fully believed it. He was terrified of the spirits' revenge. Irumbaadi and the others tried to allay his fears. They even gave him some special vibuthi to use as protection. However, in his state of extreme anxiety, Ramasamy must have mistaken some rat poison for the holy ash and consumed that instead.

"When the body is in a state of fear, poison spreads through the bloodstream faster. It works the same way with snakebite victims.

"In Ramasamy's case, he was so terrified of evil spirits that the rat poison ended up killing him. The people in the village began to suspect something was wrong. That's when the teacher started spreading the rumour that the evil spirits who haunted the hill had become restless again, and attacked Ramasamy.

"Around the same time, Deenadayalan caught hold of Chinna Pechi. Pechi trusted him; she was excited to go with him and start learning. But that's not what he wanted her for."

Raja Bhaskar paused and sipped at his coffee. "I'll tell you another thing. Deenadayalan is an expert in mesmerism!"

This news gave Rajendran a jolt.

"He hypnotized Chinna Pechi, making her wander all over the village like she was mentally affected. He made her do and say whatever he commanded. But at the same time, Ramasamy's mysterious death now had him and his partners-in-crime seriously worried that they might suffer some supernatural retribution as well. That's when they reached the conclusion that they should start offering ritual sacrifices to pacify the gods. To enable this, they called on the sorcerer Marnad. Irumbaadi and Marnad built hideouts—inside the haystacks, and on the hill—and began making preparations for the sacrifices. They caught and killed four people. Ganesan; Bangaru, the mason; Rajamanickam; and the astrologer."

Rajendran suddenly interrupted Raja Bhaskar.

"I'm sorry, sir, but there are some holes in your story. Ganesan was killed even before Ramasamy lost his life. And when the mason was killed, they didn't cut off his head—instead his body was used to make everyone believe that Irumbaadi was dead. But you're saying that these two were also offered up as sacrifices!?"

"Listen, I'm just telling you whatever Rudra told me."

"What about all those times when the spirits possessed me? I wrote so many things..."

"Wasn't the teacher right next to you every time that happened?"

"Yes."

"You were like a tool in his hands. He was skilled enough in the art of capturing minds that he could make you believe a spirit had entered you."

"But why did he do that to *me*?"

"At first he didn't think that the police would get involved. But I reached out to them and brought them in. I was the one who spoke to Rudra in Tirunelveli. The teacher didn't expect that one bit. And he didn't expect his own student Rudra to show up either. He tried to make it seem like the ghosts were responsible for everything, in order to divert the police's attention."

"Then he needn't have brought up the treasure at all! He could have just made me believe that it was all the work of the evil spirits that haunted the hill."

"That is where you need to appreciate Rudra's cleverness. The news of the treasure only broke because Rajamanickam took some of the gold to a jeweller. The teacher came to know that the jeweller had spread the news. He then realised that he couldn't keep up the evil spirits story much longer. So, he himself brought up the treasure during one of your 'conversations' with the spirits.

"As the situation in Aayakudi kept changing from day to day, Deenadayalan kept adapting his stories accordingly.

"Once Rudra arrived with his large contingent of policemen, the mood got tense. A disagreement broke out. Deenadayalan came under fire from his partners. Irumbaadi and Marnad blamed him for the police being there.

"But at the same time, they wanted to make life difficult for Rudra. They deliberately murdered the astrologer in the hopes that the S.P. would be furious and suspend Rudra immediately. Then they kidnapped Thenmozhi as well. The teacher and his other accomplice tried to stop them—but Irumbaadi and Marnad wouldn't listen. So, Deenadayalan made a decision. If he could convince Irumbaadi and Marnad to try and escape from the village, then it was likely that the police would shoot them. With those two out of the way, he and his other, still-unnamed partner could split the entire treasure between themselves. So he arranged for you to have a final conversation with the astrologer's spirit. Using that as a cover, he revealed their hiding places, as well as the spots where they had buried the heads.

"After that, everything fell into place just as he had envisioned. Before the police reached the haystacks, Deenadayalan contacted Irumbaadi and Marnad on his cell phone and told them the coast was clear for them to escape. Then he sent an SMS to Rudra—who didn't know that the teacher even had a phone—informing him about their escape plan. That's why Rudra was standing on top of the water tank. And just as the teacher expected, he shot the two of them.

"But when Rudra checked Irumbaadi and Marnad's phones, he realised that the number that had messaged them just before they ran was the same number that had given him the tip.

"But the teacher had thrown his cell phone into the well behind his house. Later, during questioning, he admitted that the number was his—a prepaid one."

"So that's how Rudra caught the teacher? The cell phone number?" Rajendran was still astonished.

The tiffin had arrived at the table and grown very cold. Raja Bhaskar hadn't touched it yet.

"No Rajendran. The reason the teacher got caught was the young girl, Chinna Pechi."

CHAPTER 26

RAJENDRAN LOOKED AT THE EDITOR quizzically.

"The SMS that Rudra had received and the SMSes that were on Marnad and Irumbaadi's phones had all come from the same number. Rudra was able to confirm that all three messages originated within Aayakudi itself. He then concluded that the person who'd sent the messages was the same person who'd been aiding and abetting the criminals all the while from within the village.

"First, he asked around and learned that the teacher did indeed own a cell phone—he had just never brought it out around you or Rudra. Then he showed up at the teacher's house unannounced, planning to ask him some questions. But the teacher wasn't at home. At that point, Rudra remembered that Chinna Pechi had been standing around the water tank earlier, so he decided to go to her house and talk to her.

"He felt that walking around the village in uniform might alert his target. So he went in disguise! Wearing a lungi and a T-shirt, and carrying a bagful of Burma umbrellas and perfumes. He walked around the village like a door-to-door salesman.

"When he reached Pechi's house and looked in through the window, what he saw left him flabbergasted! The teacher had Pechi sitting cross-legged on the floor, and he was dangling a round medallion back and forth in front of her eyes.

" 'Hey Rudrapathy! This is Ramasamy! I know where the treasure is buried. In the northeast corner of the village, there is a large rectangular rock. About ten feet from the rock is a custard apple tree. The treasure is buried at its base. The plan is to leave the loot there until all the commotion dies down and the police leave. After that, he plans to go dig it up—the person who planned all of this, a man called Velayudham. He was the one responsible for my death, but now I have had my revenge! He died a bloody death, and now he is lying in the middle of Pazhanisamy's field.

" 'Go retrieve the treasure first. Then go find Velayudham's body.

" 'Now, do you believe that the spirits are real?'

"The teacher was making Pechi repeat these words over and over, line by line. But as she was saying them, her eyes went to the window of the hut, and her gaze fell on Rudra's face. When the teacher followed her eyes to what she was staring at, he was shattered, and broke into smithereens.

"Rudra learned that the plan was to set aside about ten percent of the actual treasure to be found by the police under the custard apple tree. Then they would frame this other man, Velayudham, as a fellow conspirator of Irumbaadi and Marnad. The next step was to kill him and dump his body out in the fields.

"As the saying goes, even an elephant can lose its footing sometimes. Just like that, fate made the teacher slip and fall right in front of Rudra's eyes.

"After that, the police spoke to the teacher in their own language for a while. Soon he came out with the story I've just given you.

"That's what Rudra told me."

At last, the editor seemed to have finished his narration. Finally, he turned his attention to the cold tiffin in front of him. He tore off a small piece of the poori and popped it into his mouth.

Rajendran didn't have too many questions left after this long explanation. But there was still one important one he had to ask.

"So did the teacher have the rest of the treasure?"

The editor only chewed on his poori and watched Rajendran's face.

"Why are you just staring at me?"

"If I tell you what I have to say, you'll just stare back at me."

"Tell me, sir."

"The teacher was just an arrow. The archer is someone else."

"But who?"

"If only the teacher would give us the name, the whole case would be solved. But he won't talk!"

"But who is he trying to protect?"

"We don't know. The interrogation is still ongoing," said Raja Bhaskar. "Anyway, that's the current state of affairs. Come on, finish your poori and we'll make a move."

"I'm sure I can get the truth out of the teacher if I meet him."

"I don't know about that. If he chooses to give us the truth, then all of these riddles will be solved. But he's refusing to tell us. Apparently, he keeps saying that he's willing to die. He's asking the police to hang him to death!"

"So, the real mastermind is *still* yet to be caught."

"Not just him; the treasure as well!"

Rajendran felt exhausted. He let out a big sigh.

* * *

Rajendran's mother Sankari rushed to him and gave him a hug as he walked into the house.

"What is this, *kanna*? Don't you miss home when you're away for so long?"

"Come on, Amma! You know the kind of job I have!"

"Answer me this—are you a reporter or are you a policeman?"

"I know what you're asking. In these times, a reporter needs to be smarter and wiser than a policeman. You can even say we're a sort of 'super police'. That's the way things are these days."

"Leave all that. What is this I hear about you promising to marry some girl over there? Is it true?"

"Yes, ma, it's true. What else has the editor told you? Don't ask me questions in instalments, ask all of them together!"

"Don't act testy! A wedding is not a small matter! You know what they say… a marriage is a crop to be nurtured over a thousand years."

"Oh, I fully agree! That's why I chose not to insult that thousand-year tradition by bringing dowry, horoscope matching, religion, caste and all such nonsense into the discussion."

Sankari couldn't think of anything to say to this, so she just sighed. Then she asked, "Dey, so you're really getting married in just two days' time?"

He held her hand. "Yes, Amma. I understand why you're disappointed. You wanted to print up a lot of invitations and send them out to the entire world. You wanted me to have a big grand wedding like everyone else. But I think it's a lot more important to shut the mouths of all of these superstitious people who think Thenmozhi is unlucky, and that she'll never get married because of her horoscope. Please try and understand that, Amma."

She accepted his passionate plea. "All right. Everything will happen only as fate wills it. As long as it all turns out for the best, I am happy."

"You just stay with me and give me your full support, Amma. Only good things will happen."

Sankari hugged him tight when she heard those words. Her eyes filled with tears of joy.

* * *

Aayakudi. The house that the police had occupied.

S.P. Chidambara Rajan's Ambassador came to a halt, its siren blaring. He stepped out of the car. Rudra was at the entrance and welcomed him with a smart salute.

"So this is where our squad is staying for the time being?"

"Yes sir. Please come in and take a look."

He walked around the house and went into one of the rooms. He took a seat on a new cane chair that had been placed there for him. A junior policeman brought him some coffee in a porcelain cup. Along with it were two samosas.

As he savoured them, he looked to Rudra and said, "Congratulations!"

"Thank you, sir."

"Rudra, I won't go overboard with my praise. But I know that you and your team should be congratulated for the work you've done so far."

"I understand sir. We've prevented more murders from taking place here. But we're yet to identify the last criminal or locate the treasure. So we've only come halfway."

"As long as you understand. So, what is that teacher saying? Will he ever confess?"

"Which criminal has ever confessed everything at the start? They've been after this prize for a long time. My guess is that the treasure is worth almost a hundred crores."

"The criminal and the treasure should both come into our hands soon. If the teacher refuses to talk, then we'll make arrangements to take him to Bangalore—they have special treatments there to extract the truth."

"Sure sir. But I'm confident I can get him to talk here itself."

"All right. He's already in custody. What is he afraid of now? Is the man he's protecting really such a bigshot?"

"Give me some more time sir. I think this issue might have political connections—to a minister."

S.P. Chidambara Rajan leapt out of the cane chair. "What?"

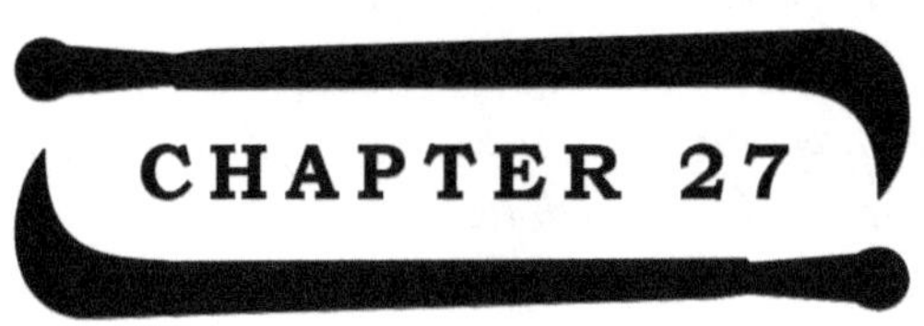

CHIDAMBARA RAJAN'S HANDS SHOOK as if he'd received an electric shock.

"Rudrapathy! What are you saying? This case started with us looking for an escaped convict. Then came the evil spirits. Next you said it was all tied to a buried treasure. Now you're telling me that there are links to a minister as well? Do you have any proof?"

"Not yet. I suspect that it's not just the minister, but some others as well, who are the reason for the teacher's continued silence."

"But the teacher hasn't opened his mouth. How did you establish a link to a minister?"

"I found some letters in the teacher's house. One of them is from an archaeologist. That man is related to the minister." Rather than say more, Rudrapathy opened a drawer, took out a file, removed a paper from it, and handed it to the S.P. It was a photocopy of a letter.

The letter was written in large, easy-to-read characters.

Dear Deenadayalan,

The questions you asked me when we met at the wedding in Tirunelveli have left me sleepless. This letter is in response to those queries. You asked about the legend in your village regarding the

Kattabomman-era treasure buried in the hill nearby. As an archaeologist, I couldn't dismiss it as mere rumour. So I looked into it further. My research revealed many shocking truths.

Pulidevan was a raja who ruled these parts many centuries ago. He refused to pay the tax that the British demanded. In response, the British attacked him, with the support of the Arcot Nawab. But Pulidevan defeated them! He'd placed a number of battalions around the Tirunelveli border, well prepared for an assault. All of them were hiding in hills or in caves, usually near some water source. They continued to train for battle while in hiding. I uncovered evidence that some of them stayed on the hill near your village as well.

You mentioned a local belief that the area is haunted. Those rumours got their start back in those days. It was a defence strategy employed by Pulidevan's men to ensure that the general public, as well as their enemies, stayed away from the places where the troops were stationed.

Whichever way you look at it, the chances of a treasure being hidden in that area are quite high. The gold could have belonged to a king like Kattabomman; or it could also have been buried by some wealthy landlords of your village to protect it from falling into the hands of the Britishers, or into the hands of thieves. It's also possible that Pulidevan's troops collected gold and money from the locals and consolidated it to procure more weaponry.

Whatever be the case, I'm confident of locating the treasure if I come to the hill. Such treasures are usually buried in places that have some kind of identifying marks. Being a trained archaeologist, I can locate such marks easily, whereas a regular person might overlook them.

I'll arrive in your village at night, so that no one else sees me. The two of us will go the hill. You mentioned this person named Rajamanickam that's usually hanging around there, involved in some criminal activity. That could actually work to our advantage. Ideally, in such matters, one shouldn't involve too many people; but sometimes establishing a coalition is the best way forward. I'll handle Rajamanickam.

Once we confirm the existence of the gold, we can work on extracting it. Normally, any such treasure automatically becomes the property of the government. You know this as well as I do. If the government catches wind of it, then all of us will be in danger. But I know a way to make sure they never get involved.

One of my relatives is a minister. He's facing a cash crunch at the moment. If we include him in our plans, he can ensure that there is no government interference… especially from the police!

I know of other archaeologists who have found such treasures, taken the gold, melted it into biscuits, and enjoyed their lives with the money. I've been waiting for such an opportunity for a long time and I don't intend to let this one slip. I'll speak to you in person to explain how we should go about it, and what precautions we need to take.

Is your daughter Malarvizhi doing well in Seranmadevi? Please write to me in detail. Actually, if you have a cell phone, that's a better mode of communication. Discussing such matters via letter is not always advisable. Please get yourself a phone if you do not have one, and from now on, we'll talk that way.

Destroy this letter after reading.

Yours
Janardhana Pandian

Chidambara Rajan finished reading the long letter and looked up, blinking his eyes.

"Your hunch seems well founded, Rudrapathy."

"I need to be very careful with every step I take sir. This Janardhana Pandian is my next target. The other criminals are probably confident that the teacher won't let any of their names slip. I'm sure they're watching to see what I do next. I need to be able to con him well!"

"You're right. I have no objections to the way you're proceeding with the investigation. Act decisively! Make sure that the final score is in our favour."

"It certainly will be sir. Despite the instruction at the end, Deenadayalan *didn't* destroy this letter. So we know that he wasn't fully honest with Janardhana Pandian. The teacher has made sure to leave himself an escape route at every stage of the scheme. Even so, he's in our custody now. If I hadn't gone to see Chinna Pechi, he would have gotten away with everything, just as he had planned! The entire issue would have been closed with Irumbaadi and Marnad. But that wasn't to be."

"Why is he refusing to talk even after being caught red-handed, though? Does he think this minister will intervene and save him?" Chidambara Rajan mused.

Rudra considered for a moment, then shook his head.

"What is it Rudra?"

"No sir. I think the teacher is well aware of how self-serving politicians can be in such situations. I think there is a larger threat behind his silence."

"What sort of a threat, though?"

"That's what I'm trying to understand, too. We can beat him up during interrogation, even send him to the gallows to be hanged to death. But what is he still worried about? Who is he afraid of?"

"Whatever it is, it's not something you and I can figure out in a half-hour conversation. The teacher is very intelligent, but fate was not on his side. I hope it stays on ours." Rudrapathy paused. "There's another important thing."

"What's that, Rudra?"

"By now, everyone will know we have the teacher in custody—this archaeologist, Janardhana Pandian... and through him, the minister. Also, the other mystery conspirator, who we suspect is still somewhere in the village. All of them must also be confident by this time that the teacher isn't going to name any of them. But they still must be wondering what's coming next."

"Exactly. So, what do you plan to do about it?"

"We should wrap up the case quickly. Name the teacher as the sole accused."

"I don't understand what you're saying."

"Bring the whole investigation to a close, the way the teacher wanted us to… as if I hadn't caught him with Chinna Pechi at all."

"You mean…?"

"Their plan was to reveal one small portion of the treasure, put the blame on Velayudham, and have him killed. The teacher has already admitted his guilt. He's also revealed where the treasure is—I mean the ten percent of the treasure that they had agreed to give up to us. We'll retrieve that portion of the treasure and hand it over to the government. The case will start working its way through the courts and the teacher will be punished as per the law. That's the plan sir."

"And while everyone believes that this is what is happening, you will continue to pursue the others."

"Yes sir."

"Like I said earlier—act bravely and proceed as you see fit. I'm giving you full freedom."

"Thank you, sir. Why don't you come with me right now and have a word with the teacher? Bring things to a conclusion."

"Sure. Where is he now?"

Two minutes later, the S.P. and Rudra stood in front of Deenadaya-lan. He sat with his head bowed down, his hands in cuffs.

"Aiyya…" Rudra called out to him respectfully. He slowly lifted his head. His eyes showed a combination of shame and fear.

"Aiyya, the S.P. has come to a decision. I told him what you've said, that you're ready to give up your life before you give up the truth. Well, we've decided we don't really need to know that truth. We don't want this to go all the way up to Ministers and MLAs. He's asked me to make you the prime accused and close the case. He has a lot of pressure from above."

A new light gleamed in the teacher's eyes.

"As per your original plan, we will take a part of the treasure, put it in a pot and hand it over to the courts along with you. We'll file the FIR so that it makes things easy for you to eventually escape conviction. The S.P. feels that will be sufficient to close the case out."

As Rudra finished, a sudden brightness—*gubeer!*—came over the teacher's face.

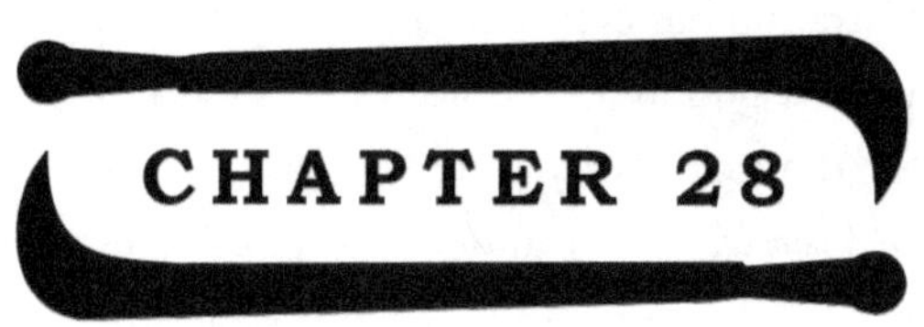

CHAPTER 28

The S.P. looked on as Rudra drew the teacher into their trap. For a moment, it seemed like he was about to fall in. But then his mouth twisted into a wry smile.

The smile irritated Rudra. "What, sir? Why are you smiling like that?"

"What else should I do, Rudrapathy? Did you think I'd be happy? Did you imagine that just because you mentioned pressure from the ministerial level, I'd believe I could go free? If so, then my condolences to you. To be quite honest with you, there are no ministers involved in this matter at all. I promise," the teacher said, and began to cry loudly.

They could see him go through a number of mental battles in a short time. They waited expectantly to see what he would tell them next. He finished crying and began to speak again.

"Rudrapathy... Don't keep grilling me. I have eaten his salt—I am a very loyal person. But I will tell you a few things. I know you saw the letter Janardhana Pandian sent me. But I never sent him a reply.

"I had initially planned on including Jana in our plans, but then I rejected the idea. There are many reasons for that. I won't go into those details now. But if you believe that Jana is involved in any of this, you should change that opinion.

"My partner and I worked hard for many years to find that treasure. I couldn't bear the thought of the government taking control of it.

"No administration has ever done a single good thing for this village. Our water supply is polluted, our electricity supply is erratic, there are no hospitals for the sick. Every time we make a request, all we get in response is 'We'll see what we can do.' And nothing ever gets done. No, from the beginning, I've been dead set against handing over the treasure to the government.

"Another thing you should note is that we didn't *steal* anything from anyone. It's been sitting right there in the ground for centuries. By all rights it should be used to benefit the village! If everything had gone according to plan, my partner and I would have distributed the entire treasure to the people of Aayakudi and used it for the betterment of the place. The only person who thought differently was that hot-headed rascal Rajamanickam! You remember that necklace he gave Thenmozhi? That piece was part of the treasure. He's the one who took some of the coins to the jeweller, too. It's only because of him that you police got involved. That's why we had to get rid of him. Listen, there's been a good reason for every death in this village. There are no selfish motives here, Rudrapathy. Not even a little bit."

Rudra listened with surprise. There was plenty in the teacher's fiery speech that was new to him.

The teacher continued.

"Even now, I'm not sad I've been caught. Because everything I did, I did for the good of the village. I'm well aware that if I told you who my partner is and where the treasure is hidden, I could get my sentence reduced to a few years at most. But I'm not going to do it. Regardless of what happens to me, I want my partner to succeed. I repeat: that treasure belongs to the village! You cannot take it away. My partner will never be caught, and you'll never get your hands on the gold and jewels either. You and your team will just spend years going around in circles.

"We've made countless requests for a police station over the years, but nothing ever happened. Now, all of a sudden, we have one right in the middle of the village. You'll maintain the station here at least until the treasure is found. And in that time, Aayakudi will get a lot of relief from the thieves who come for our cattle, our goats, and our harvest.

"But one thing is certain, Rudrapathy. You will not taste any further victory in my village. My prayers are that you never do."

The S.P. cut in. "Rudrapathy, I don't think there's any use in going on talking to this fellow. Try whatever techniques you need to use—from electric shocks to the Punjab beating. I think when he gets one of those, he'll automatically vomit up all of the secrets he has hidden away in his mind," roared Chidambara Rajan.

The teacher didn't even flinch. He placed his handcuffed hands on his lap, looked at Rudra and said, "Rudrapathy, can you come here for a minute?"

Rudra continued standing where he was, a few feet away.

"Come here, *pa*. Let me tell you a little secret, for your ears only."

Still, Rudrapathy didn't move.

"Your vaadhyar is calling you! Come!"

"No, sir!" said Rudra. "Please stop trying to distract us with your extremist talk. Up till this moment, I've continued to look at you as my Tamil vaadhyar. I've never laid a finger on you… it's always been one of the others. I've stood aside consciously. Please don't spoil that respect I have for you."

"No Rudrapathy. I am really proud of you. When you dress up like a dog, you have to bark. You're only performing your duty. What you're doing is right. I too, tried to do my duty. But before I could complete it, fate intervened."

"Hunting for the treasure, trying to keep it from the government—none of those are really serious crimes, sir. But all those lives that were lost, one after the other! What of them?"

"Rudra, even today, soldiers are being shot dead on our borders. Lives lost in a battle shouldn't be counted as murders. They're sacrifices. We had to make some sacrifices to ensure the greater good. That's all."

"Aiyya... don't try and play around with words," said Rudra, walking up to him angrily, glaring. "I'm running out of patience." He stood close enough that the teacher could feel his breath on his face.

On Rudra's hip was his fully loaded service revolver, its handle sticking out of the holster.

Without ever breaking eye contact, the teacher swiftly moved his cuffed hands forward and grabbed the revolver. It all happened in a fraction of a second.

S.P. Chidambara Rajan shouted, "Rudra! Watch out!'

But it was too late. The teacher buried the muzzle of the revolver into his own chest and pulled the trigger. A bullet shot through his body with its characteristic speed.

No one had expected this!

"See, Rudrapathy?" the teacher mumbled, as he collapsed onto the table. "I'm a sacrifice, too."

The next second, his life fluttered away into the sky, like a dove.

Rudrapathy wanted to scream and cry.

* * *

The minibus screeched to a halt. Rajendran and his mother Sankari stepped off. As she got down, Sankari looked around the village.

A police jeep and an ambulance rushed past them.

Naicker had sent a few of his farm workers to meet them at the bus stop. They quickly ran up to them, took Rajendran's suitcase from his hand, and bowed deeply. "Vanakkam, thambi! Vanakkam, amma!"

"Amma, these people work for Naicker. This is Naatraayan," Rajendran said. Then he addressed them. "What was that ambulance doing here? Did something bad happen today? Has someone died?"

They remained silent.

"I'm asking you, tell me."

"Never mind all that, thambi. There are auspicious events about to start. You're the mappillai. No bad news should reach your ears."

"So something *has* happened! What? To whom? Tell me!"

"Oh, all right, thambi... You know that our Tamil vaadhyar was arrested by the police? Well, during the enquiry, it seems that he grabbed the inspector's pistol and shot himself."

"What!? The teacher is dead?" The news was a tremendous shock to Rajendran.

"Yes thambi... The whole village is over on South Street by the police station. Even the press and the TV people are here. There's a big crowd."

Before the man finished talking, Rajendran had set off towards the police station. "Amma, you go home with them," he said. "I'll be there in a while."

CHAPTER 29

RAJENDRAN RAN FAST, ANXIOUS to find out more about the teacher's suicide. Naicker's people saw him go and slapped their heads in frustration.
But Sankari was confused.

"Where is he going? Do you know?"

"He must be going to talk to that police inspector. But what's the use
of meeting anyone now?" one of them sighed.

"What do you mean? What are you talking about?" Sankari continued questioning them as they walked towards Naicker's house.

"Didn't your son tell you anything about what's been happening here
in Aayakudi?"

"He told me a little bit. But I couldn't make much sense of it."

"Better not to trouble yourself. To tell you the truth we're not sure we
know what's going on ourselves."

"I heard from Rajendran's magazine editor that the person behind all
the crimes was a Tamil teacher. Is that the same person who just committed suicide?"

"Yes. He's the one who knew all the secrets. Now he's gone, and all the
secrets have gone with him."

"Oh... So it's like the old saying: after the rain stops, the drizzle
continues."

"We're not even sure the rain has stopped yet."

As Sankari walked through the streets talking, a few of the village folk stopped to watch them. One joker was walking with an upturned basket on his head. He was curious about Sankari.

"Dey, Naatraaya! Who is this new person? Is she the nurse who's come to give people cholera injections?" he shouted.

Naatraayan was annoyed at the question. "Shut your mouth and keep walking, old man! Can't you tell the difference between Naicker's in-laws and the cholera nurse?"

Several other people heard this response, and a number of heads turned to look at Sankari. She heard them whisper among themselves, "Oh! She's the mother of the boy that Thenmozhi is going to marry." "Look… it's Thenu's mother-in-law…"

Sankari understood at once the respect Naicker's family had in the village.

* * *

Rajendran ran into the police station, gasping for breath. Rudra stood there rubbing his temples.

"Sir…"

"Come Rajendran, sit down."

"I'm all right, sir. But… the teacher…"

"You must have seen the ambulance on your way here? The body's gone for post-mortem."

"What is this horrible news, sir?… Was it really the teacher who was behind everything?" asked Rajendran as he sat down on a bench across from Rudra.

"Unbelievable, no?"

"Yes sir. I can't seem to digest it."

"You're a young man. This is probably the first time you've been betrayed like this. But in my career, it's nothing new. You know, I suspected him from the very first day… and yet, at the same time, do you know how many times I prayed to God that he be found innocent?" The sorrow in Rudra's voice overflowed like froth from a bottle of beer.

"What are you going to do next, sir?"

"I don't know. The teacher committed suicide using my service revolver. My department will probably suspend me."

"Sir! But if you get suspended, what will happen to the case?"

"Oh, Rajendran, the whole police department doesn't depend entirely on Officer Rudrapathy. There are plenty of others who are much more capable than I am."

"That may be sir, but suspending you is a big mistake!"

"No, Rajendran, it's the only right thing to do. The law mustn't be influenced by emotions. It has to proceed according to a set of rules. Only then can the police carry out their duties effectively."

"How can you say this yourself, sir? Aren't you sad?"

"Why do you ask me that? Up until now I never faced defeat in even a single case in my career. But this one has been a 100% failure. I think of my suspension as the proper reward."

"I don't know whether to praise you or feel sorry for you."

"Let it be Rajendran. You're about to get married! And that will be a victory both for you and for the girl, who's seen all her engagements up till now end in shambles. You're a credit to your profession." Rudra's praise was genuine and wholehearted.

"But sir…"

"I mean it. Stop worrying about me. Has your mother come with you?"

"Yes, sir."

"Other relatives?"

"I don't have a very large family, sir. One uncle and one sister. Both of them will arrive with their families tomorrow."

"And the wedding is the day after?"

"I think so. I haven't gone to Naicker's house yet. I saw the ambulance as soon as I got off the bus. I asked about it, they told me what happened, and I ran straight here."

"You haven't even seen them yet? Right, you get going then. I'll come along with you. You aren't leaving that house again until the wedding is over with. Come on!"

"Don't worry sir. Nothing will happen to me. Everything has come to an end now…" Rajendran spoke very casually, but Rudra's face immediately tightened.

"What is it sir?"

"Sorry Rajendran. Nothing has come to an end here. Don't forget that."

"What are you saying sir?"

"Before the murders, the treasure was buried somewhere in the village. But now it's been transferred into someone else's custody. And whoever is safeguarding it is the man behind all of these troubles. He probably thinks that now that the teacher has killed himself, he has escaped. But he'll still be focused on you and me.

"Rajendran, up until now, you've been a reporter. But tomorrow, you're marrying into Aayakudi. You're going to become one of them."

"So?"

"So he'll be watching you very closely."

"You think that this person is planning to kill me as well?"

"Yes, I do."

"Then why don't you use me as bait, and catch the rat in a trap!?"

As soon as Rajendran spoke, Rudra rose and clasped his shoulders.

"Thank you Rajendran! I'm so happy to hear you say that so fearlessly. But so many innocent lives have already been lost. I don't want to lose another. I'd rather have the crook get away than to put you at risk. You're going to be Thenmozhi's husband now. That poor girl! She doesn't need any more tragedies. Keep that in mind."

Moved by Rudra's generosity, Rajendran began tearing up.

Both of them got into the jeep that was parked outside and headed towards Naicker's house.

"Sir, you must attend the wedding for certain."

"I got permission from the S.P. a long time ago. We've made arrangements for police protection, too, so that the wedding proceeds smoothly. I'm in charge of that. You might say I'm your police escort from this moment on."

"Sir!"

"It'll be my pleasure, Rajendran."

"And what about afterwards?"

"Like I told you earlier; I'll go to Tirunelveli, receive my suspension order, and go back to my home town."

"And what will happen to this case?"

"It'll get assigned to someone else. But listen—you and Thenmozhi should head straight to Chennai after the wedding! You mustn't stay on here in the village for any reason."

Rajendran agreed to do as Rudra said. The jeep stopped in front of Naicker's grill gate. Thenmozhi was peering out expectantly from the window of the house.

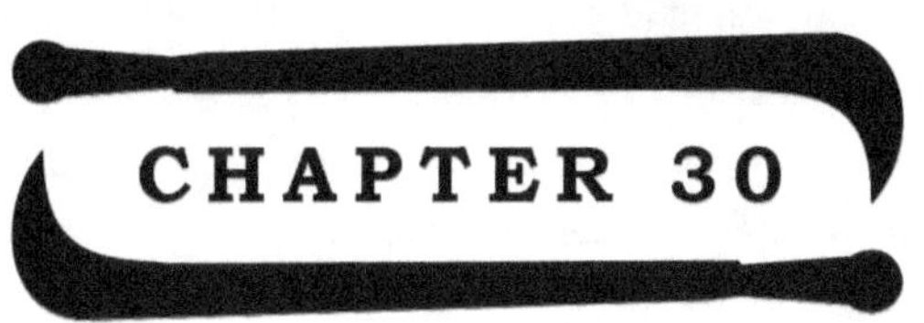

CHAPTER 30

EVERY MEMBER OF NAICKER'S HOUSEHOLD had their eyes glued to Rajendran and Rudra as they got down from the jeep. As soon as they entered, Naicker ran out to greet them. "Welcome! Welcome!" his voice rang out loudly. Thenmozhi watched happily, a bridal glow shining from her face.

Rudrapathy greeted Naicker in return.

"What is this, sir! Looks like you've brought the mappillai home yourself!" Naicker said to the policeman, jovially.

There were many chairs laid out in the front yard. Naicker's extended family had arrived for the wedding and were sitting around chatting. Rajendran, Rudrapathy, and Naicker sat down among them.

Rudrapathy laughed. "I'm Rajendran's best man!"

"Well said! Why don't you get him a job in your department while you're at it?" said one of Naicker's cousins sitting nearby.

"If Rajendran is ready, why not? We'll get him posted right here in Aayakudi!" said Rudra without missing a beat.

Even as he sat there chatting, Rudrapathy's instructions were being carried out in the area surrounding the house. A dozen policemen were walking the perimeter in civilian clothes. They were all watching carefully to ensure that nothing unforeseen would occur. All of them were aware of Rudra's fear that Rajendran might be the next target.

Meanwhile, Rajendran's mother Sankari was enjoying the elaborate hospitality inside the house. Vanjiammal was personally attending to her. A Pathamadai mat was laid out in front of her, and on top of it were spread out all of Thenmozhi's wedding saris, her jewellery, and the thaali.

"We bought all of these things a long time ago. Finally, the time has come for them to be worn!" said Vanjiammal.

Sankari was eager to meet Thenmozhi and speak to her at length. "All of this is very nice, for sure! But when do I get to meet my future daughter-in-law?" she asked.

"Aiyyo! Of course, you must be anxious to see her. Come with me," said Vanjiammal, walking towards Thenmozhi's room. Sankari followed her.

As she walked, her eyes glanced outside. Rajendran was sitting next to Naicker, talking to him. The sight of Rudra's imposing figure, standing near them in uniform, caught her eye. Something about the picture bothered her, and her expression changed.

As soon as she entered the room, Vanjiammal quietly posed the question: "Are you wondering why the police are here?"

"Yes."

"He's the person who put a stop to the murders that were happening in our village. It was he and our mappillai who were responsible for everything."

"Oh, is it!" said Sankari, breathing deeply.

When Thenmozhi met her soon-to-be mother-in-law Sankari for the first time, their eyes locked and drew one another in. It was the first heartbeat of a relationship that would last for many years.

"Fall at her feet and ask for her blessings," said Vanjiammal. As Thenmozhi did so, Sankari cracked her knuckles against her forehead to ward off the evil eye. Multiple popping sounds were audible.

"So many people have cast an eye on her!" Sankari exclaimed.

"Indeed. We were so worried… we thought she would never get a thaali around her neck."

"Well, don't you worry about anything from now on. She's already my daughter-in-law. The ceremony and the thaali are just to announce it to society."

"Amma, you have a very generous heart!" said Vanjiammal.

"Even if I had been against it, my son would surely have disregarded my words. He cares about your daughter a lot."

Thenmozhi's eyes welled up with tears.

"I'm so glad to hear it," said Vanjiammal. "Maybe fate wanted my daughter to find such a good husband. Maybe that's why none of the earlier arrangements worked out."

"It must be the truth. When fate has decided that two people are meant to be together, who are we to challenge it?"

As Vanjiammal and Sankari spoke their minds, Thenmozhi stepped away from them and went towards the window. She stood there watching Rajendran as he and the other people sitting outside talked animatedly. At that moment, her father was telling the others something—speaking just loudly enough for her to make out their words.

"Mr. Policeman," Naicker was saying to Rudrapathy, "I have prayed to every single God to ensure that this wedding goes through without any troubles. As soon as the ceremony is over, I am going to take the bride and groom with me to Chennai. I've just purchased a house in the city."

Rajendran looked taken aback by this. Rudra, understanding what was on his mind, asked his question for him.

"But why are you in such a hurry?"

"Hurry? You don't know my fears!"

"But I'm right here at your side," said Rudrapathy. "What do you have to be scared of?"

"Please don't take this the wrong way. But the astrologer got murdered while you were right here in Aayakudi. Were you able to do anything to prevent it?"

"You're worried that the killer will attend the wedding and target Rajendran? Is that it?"

"Of course. I'm sure you've also heard the talk around the village."

"What are they saying?"

"Some of them blame Rajendran for bringing the police here, and for all the unfortunate things that happened. I've been asked if I really think marrying my daughter to such a man is the right thing to do."

"And what did you say to them?"

"I told them my son-in-law had only done good things for us. But they didn't agree. They think the vaadhyar and his partner would have distributed the treasure among everyone in the village. I could tell they're disappointed now that it won't happen."

"But we still don't know who the teacher's partner was. Whoever it is, he can still distribute the gold among the villagers if he wants to."

"Not without revealing his identity. He'd get caught."

"He could wait for a while, until everything quiets down."

"He could. Or he could make a getaway and keep it all for himself. Nothing is certain."

"Essentially, you believe that he is not going to fall into the hands of the police. Right?'

"Yes. News of what the vaadhyar said before he killed himself has spread all around the village. No one views him as a criminal. Everyone's sad that he died the way he did. Now even if they do come to know who his partner is, no one here will give him up."

"Mr. Naicker, you're the panchayat president. Would *you* give him up?"

"Certainly. But I'm worried that he'll do harm to me first."

"Why would he target you?"

"Why do you think? Here I am sitting and talking to the man who wants to arrest him. My own son-in-law is preparing to write pages and pages about him in his magazine. And now Rajendran will be coming and going to and from this village as he pleases, because it's his in-laws' place. All this must have made a complete mess of all his plans, and I'm sure he's looking to take out his anger."

"So that's why you were in a great hurry to find a place in Chennai?"

"Yes. I paid an advance through a broker just yesterday. My daughter and her husband will have their first night in that house in the city."

Although Naicker explained that he was being fearful and cautious, Rajendran did not like what he was hearing. His face made his feelings very clear.

"Why do you look like that, Rajendran? Don't you agree with this?" asked Rudra sharply.

"No, sir, I don't. After the wedding, I wish to stay right here in the village. I want to help convert your defeat into a victory. To tell you the truth, I *hope* this man targets me. Only then will I learn who he is."

"What if he doesn't come after you? What if he just silently slips away with the treasure?"

"Wouldn't that outcome be good for the village, too? It's in their best interests to no longer have a criminal in their midst." "Enough, sir," Naicker cut in, putting an end to their discussion. "I'm done thinking about the well-being of the village. What I care about is my daughter's future. And if she is to have a good life, then my son-in-law must also have a good life. So, after the wedding, they can go lead it together in the city. That's all I want."

Thenmozhi, who had been watching all of this through the window, felt her heart thumping—*bak bak!*

CHAPTER 31

"Come, thambi," Naicker went on. "I've gone through all this trouble of buying a house in Chennai just so you and my daughter can be comfortable. The broker said that the price was perhaps a lakh or two on the higher side, but I didn't care… I just want you two to have a nice place. Each moment you stay here in Aayakudi is only making me more and more anxious."

Rudra appeared to agree with him. Sankari caught wind of the conversation and joined in.

"You make it sound like my son is imminent danger."

"Yes. I think it's best for your son to be completely disconnected from this village. The police are here now; they can handle the rest of it. It's between them and the criminal. Who are we to stand between them?"

"That makes sense. Rajendra, why are you being so stubborn about staying here?"

"I'm not being stubborn. It's just that, however it happened, I got involved in this whole issue. And it hasn't yet come to a conclusion. It would be shameful now for me to run away like I've got nothing to do with it."

"There's no shame in it at all! Why do you think like that? The police are here, no? They'll take care of everything, da. If you see a lizard running away from you, why try to catch it and put it on your head?"

"Okay ma, suppose you're right. But how do we know the criminal won't find me in Chennai?"

"You can simply step away from this whole matter and forget about it. I'm sure nothing will happen. But if you stay here, it'll disturb the criminal who's now in hiding. He'll be worried that you'll try to discover his identity, so he'll try and get rid of you. Why invite trouble?"

As Naicker and Sankari took turns at him, Rajendran looked like he might be slowly coming around. Rudra noticed this and decided to put a full stop to the whole controversy.

"Rajendran, as a reporter, you've already fulfilled your duties. You've gone a step further and you are giving a girl a new lease on life. Do you want Thenmozhi to have a bright future or don't you?"

Rajendran took a moment to respond. "Sir, my Thenmozhi and I will live a good life. You keep assuming that the criminal is going to kill me… Don't you have any faith that I might figure out who he is before he does so?"

"Well, this is the first time I've ever tasted defeat in a case. If a man commits a crime for selfish reasons, it's easy enough to catch him and punish him. But if he has the support of a group, an entire community, then it takes a lot of luck and a lot of time. This criminal who's gone into hiding with the Aayakudi treasure could turn out to be another Veerappan, if everyone here refuses to tell the police anything!

"But from now on," Rudra continued firmly, "not another word from you about the criminal or the treasure. Your treasure is right there!" he pointed his index finger up to the window, at Thenmozhi.

Thenmozhi looked at Rajendran with nervous anticipation. Seeing that he seemed convinced by Rudra's words, she sighed in relief—"*Appaada!*"

* * *

The next morning!

The street in front of Naicker's house was nearly split in two by the sound of the loudspeakers. The entire street had been closed off, and a large thatch roof had been erected. From each one of the posts holding up the roof, a variety of plants and flowers had been hung. Hundreds of steel chairs were neatly arranged beneath.

Naicker had invited the entire village of Aayakudi to be present at the wedding. Arrangements for food had been made in the large open ground that was usually used to dry and bundle up harvested rice. A feast was being prepared with mutton curry for everyone! Eighty goats had been procured for the occasion; they had all been tied up in nearby fields, where about twenty men were busy at work cutting off their heads and skinning them.

The blood from the goats flowed copiously across the fields, attracting a large number of flies. As if that were not enough, crows began to gather by the dozens as well.

The police, still doing their rounds in civilian clothes, kept their eyes on all of this.

Thenmozhi was getting her make-up done inside her room.

"Look at you, Thenu!" gushed a middle-aged friend of the family. "You've never even travelled as far as Tirunelveli to watch a movie, have you? And now you're going to get married and move to the big city! It goes to show… when it rains, it really pours!"

Thenmozhi smiled, blushing.

Rudra slowly walked around the entire wedding area, surveying everything. Naicker and his wife Vanjiammal appeared to be floating in a pool of their own tears of joy. Sankari was seated next to the stage, watching the proceedings around her with rapt attention.

Hundreds of people had come for the wedding. People from every home had dressed up in their brightest colours. The crowds stretched all around Naicker's house.

A number of Tata Sumos and Ambassadors were parked here and there. Several political leaders, of a few different party affiliations, were in attendance.

Chinna Pechi was there too, dressed in new clothes and holding her mother's hand. She finally looked like a happy young girl.

Many of the guests were astonished to see Deenadayalan's daughter, Malarvizhi, and his son-in-law, Brigadeesan. Brigadeesan wore a bright red shirt and a white veshti, dressed up like any of the other attendees. It had only been a few days since the teacher had shot himself. The two of them had come to Aayakudi to collect the body from the police and to perform the funeral rites.

They were now seated in one of the rows of chairs facing the stage. Brigadeesan's bright red shirt caught Rudra's eye. He called one of his men over and whispered something to him. Rajendran observed them from the stage.

"Who is that fellow in the red shirt?"

"He is the dead teacher's son-in-law, sir."

"Did Naicker invite him to the wedding?"

"It appears so, sir. He wouldn't be here without an invitation, all dressed up like that."

"Don't give me your guesses as answers. I need to know if they were invited by Naicker. Find out any way you can …"

"Yes sir!" The policeman stepped away with a nod of his head.

Naicker, who had noticed this conversation, walked over to Rudra.

"What is it sir, any trouble?"

"Oh nothing, Naicker Aiyya… just a regular chat with my people. No trouble at all. I brought a gift for the bride and the groom; I asked him to bring it here." Having sent the Naicker on his way, Rudra sat back, one leg crossed over the other.

The auspicious hour was nearing.

The thaali was being taken around the hall to be blessed by the gathered relatives and villagers. Finally, it reached the stage.

Rajendran picked up the two ends of the sacred thread, and—accompanied by a blast of sound from the nadhaswaram and the roar of the thavil—tied it around Thenmozhi's neck. The entire village stood up to bless them. Rudra happily joined in, throwing a handful of flowers. Then he walked up and hugged Rajendran tightly to congratulate him. He took out two rings from his pocket, and put one on Rajendran's finger and the other on Thenmozhi's.

"Sir, what's all this for?" protested Rajendran.

"Oh, don't mention it, Rajendran. It's just a small token of my appreciation for your courage, sacrifice and forward thinking."

Rudra turned to leave, but stopped. He looked back at Rajendran with a smile on his face and said, "I might have another gift for you before the day is gone."

Rajendran understood what Rudra was getting at and called out to stop him. "Sir!"

His eyes were filled with questions about Rudra's "gift".

"You don't worry about that right now, Rajendran. You should be paying all your attention to her, now," Rudra said, pointing at Thenmozhi. Then he quickly walked away.

The nadhaswaram and thavil players continued playing. Their music over the loudspeakers was making the entire village vibrate. It no longer seemed the same place that had been shaken by multiple murders.

Rudra walked towards the entrance where the *thamboolam* bags were all piled up. Each bag had Rajendran's and Thenmozhi's names printed on it. A few members of Naicker's household were busy arranging the bags into two piles while another sat at a table writing and checking something in a notebook.

Curious, Rudra decided to take a closer look.

On seeing Rudra approach, one of the people who had been sorting the bags smiled and reached for a bag to give him. Naicker, who had noticed this from afar, came rushing up.

"Sir, what is this? Why are you already here, taking your thamboolam bag? You can't leave so soon! I'm sure you haven't eaten yet. Come, there's some excellent mutton curry. Please come with me and eat first!"

He ushered Rudra away towards the dining area. Then someone called out to Naicker, asking him to come up on stage to complete some wedding rituals. Naicker turned back to Rudra to insist once more that he go and eat, and then headed to the stage.

Rudra didn't go to the dining area, though. Instead, he doubled back to the entrance. Something about those piles of thamboolam bags didn't sit right with him. He asked one of the people standing near them, "Why are there two piles here?"

"All the bags on this side are for the residents of Aayakudi. That pile is for the people from outside the village," the man replied.

"And why is that?"

"I don't know, sir. I'm just following the instructions I've been given."

Rudra flipped through the notebook on the table.

"What's in this notebook?"

"The names of all the families in the village, sir. We've been told to make sure that everyone receives their thamboolam bag. So we made a list to keep track."

Rudra opened up one of the bags from the first pile. Inside were some betel leaves, areca nuts, bananas, turmeric, kumkum, and a coconut.

Then he picked up a bag from the other pile and put his hand inside. What he pulled out was a gold coin—shaped like a bajji! It was made of antique gold, with rough edges and unclear markings. It easily weighed eight grams.

And the bag in his hand held four more of them!

Rudra allowed himself a quiet smile. He instructed his men who were standing nearby, "Load up all these bags in the police jeep. Take them to the station and stand guard. I will be there shortly."

He turned to the man who was distributing them.

"Please make arrangements for alternate bags to replace these."

Rudra continued scanning the area. The teacher's son-in-law, the man in the red shirt, was nowhere to be seen. He called out to the officer he had spoken to earlier.

"I had asked you to find out about the teacher's son-in-law. What happened?"

"Sir, apparently Naicker went to their house himself to personally invite him."

"He isn't here anymore. He seems to have slipped away. Didn't you keep an eye on him?"

"There are four of us watching him sir. He's gone to the teacher's house now."

"Keep a close watch. I don't want a hint of trouble starting until Rajendran and Thenmozhi reach Chennai."

"Right sir." The officer saluted and left.

Rudra dialled S.P. Chidambara Rajan.

"Yes, Rudra."

"I've recovered the other 90% of the treasure, sir."

"Oh really?"

"Yes, sir. And I've also identified the criminal."

"Who? Who is it, Rudra?"

"He is one man. But there are a couple more assisting him."

"You're confusing me."

"You can't suspend me now sir. I am fortunate! All of my hunches proved right, and everything fell right into place."

"Did he really just fall into your hands like that?"

"Even now he believes that he cannot be caught. And he's still doing his best to misguide me."

"Careful Rudra... you might miss your target if you wait too long."

"No sir. Impossible! I wanted to make sure that there was no hindrance to Rajendran and Thenmozhi's wedding."

"Is the ceremony over?"

"Yes sir. One good deed is done. The next good deed is to handcuff that criminal."

"But who is he? The one who has been in hiding all this while?"

Rudra replied very softly, his voice nearly drowned by the sounds around him. The S.P. was shocked!

* * *

Tirunelveli Junction.

The wedding party had gathered in front of the AC coach of the Nellai Express. Rajendran was resplendent in his silk shirt and veshti; Thenmozhi looked angelic in her silk sari, bedecked with jewellery. A large crowd had come to see her off.

Rajendran, confident that Rudra would show up, kept looking out for him... and Rudra did not disappoint. As he walked through the crowd towards the newlyweds, his face showed a sense of accomplishment.

Rajendran and Rudra stepped to one side to talk.

"What Rajendran? All good to go?"

"That much you can see, no, sir? But what about you... Are you waiting for me to leave before you go hunting?"

"You could say that. Actually, I'm a little surprised there hasn't been a reaction yet."

"A reaction? To what?"

"We recovered the rest of the treasure."

"What! How?"

"It was all inside the thamboolam bags that were to be distributed at your wedding!"

"Oh no! Does that mean the criminal is someone in Thenmozhi's household?"

"Don't jump to conclusions. The killer wanted to use your wedding as an opportunity to distribute the gold among the villagers. But I sniffed it out and stopped it… and confiscated everything."

"And he didn't try to stop you?"

"He didn't have a choice! He couldn't have protested without revealing who he was. There was nothing he could do but try to lose himself in the crowd of the guests."

"Do you think you'll be able to catch him?"

"You'll probably get to know by tomorrow. First make your honeymoon plans with Thenmozhi."

"Oh, honeymoon-ponymoon. I want to know who he is!"

"Don't worry, I'm very close. You're no longer in danger. You can come visit your in-laws whenever you want. You can even go take a walk on the hill and remember old times," said Rudra, laughing.

The railway guard blew his whistle.

Inside the coach were Sankari, Vanjiammal, and a few other relatives. Naicker had remained in Aayakudi, saying he would come to Chennai in a few days. He had a lot of wedding-related work to wrap up.

The train started moving.

Rajendran stood at the door waving goodbye to everyone, but especially to Rudra.

Soon, though, everyone had receded into the distance. Rajendran walked back into the compartment with a slightly heavy heart.

Thenmozhi's gaze was fixed on him. Silently, she asked him with her eyes:

At last! Now will you finally pay some attention to me?

And silently, Rajendran answered her:

From now on, that's my only job.

Her face blushed a shade of pink that perfectly matched the sunset sky outside the train.

* * *

Rudra walked out of the station and got into his vehicle. The jeep pounced.

"Head straight to Aayakudi!"

His cell phone buzzed. As soon as he put it against his ear, a shocked expression came over his face.

"Sir, the suspect has hanged himself. The body is still swinging from the rope. Can I cut him down?" came the question from the other end.

"No, I'll be there right away. Was there a note?"

"Yes, sir."

"Read it out." Rudra's heart was beating rapidly.

My greetings to Rudrapathy; and my heartiest congratulations as well.

I understand now what fate is. It is clear to me that I cannot escape.

Rather than get caught and face the death penalty, I have decided to take the honourable way out and hang myself. My death, in a way, is an idealist's death. By the time you see this letter, I will be dead. But I repeat again—that gold belongs to my village. The government does not deserve any of it.

The policeman finished reading the letter. On the other end of the line, Rudra was punching himself.

The jeep hurtled across the road at high speed. Finally, it stopped in front of the house where the body was hanging.

The celebratory air that the wedding had brought to the village had been replaced by a deep, mournful quiet. Every house, every doorway seemed to have silent eyes that watched him.

Rudrapathy surveyed the surroundings and entered the house. He walked in and looked up at the body.

Dangling from the rope, with the tongue sticking out and the eyes popping from their sockets, was the body of Govinda Naicker.

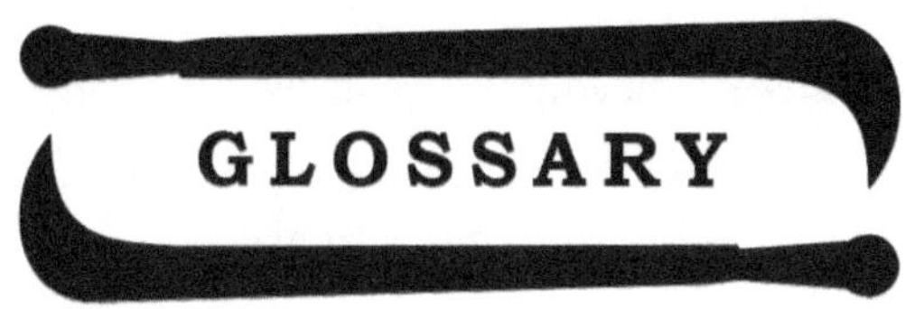

GLOSSARY

aavani

a month in the Tamil calendar, corresponding to August-September

aatha

literally, mother; can be used as a respectful address to any woman

adiye

informal address to a woman

aiyya

respectful address to a man, usually one's senior

aippasi

a month in the Tamil calendar, corresponding to October-November

aiyyo, aiyyaiyyo

a multi-purpose exclamation or mild curse

akka

elder sister, or respectful address to a slightly older woman

amma

mother

anna

elder brother, or respectful address to a slightly older man

appa

father

asura

demonic creature from Hindu mythology

Glossary

dayakattai
  a board game played with dice, similar to pachisi and ludo
dey
  informal or disrespectful address to a man
di
  informal or disrespectful address to a woman
dosham
  a flaw caused by a planet's position in the horoscope
gopuram
  a tower at the entrance to a temple
josiyar
  astrologer, fortune teller; "josiyare" is used to address such a person
kaathu karuppu
  literally "black wind"; an evil spirit
kakoos
  latrine
kanna
  dear
kumkum
  sacred red powder given in temples
ma
  informal address, usually to a woman
maama
  maternal uncle, sister's husband, or father's sister's husband
maamoi
  another form of "maama"
mannankatti
  lump of dirt (used as a mild curse)

mappillai

bridegroom, son-in-law

muhurtham

a division of time equal to forty-eight minutes; here, used to denote
an auspicious time

naataamai

village headman

nadhaswaram

a large double-reed instrument, traditionally played at weddings

pa

informal address, usually to a man

pavadai

skirt-like garment worn by girls

pey

ghost, evil spirit

pirandai

an edible creeper; sometimes called the veldt grape or devil's backbone

podalanga

snake gourd (used as a mild curse)

puli saaru

tamarind and chili broth

pulla

affectionate address to a woman

rava

semolina

romba

very, a lot

rudraksha

a sacred seed used as a prayer bead

saami

literally, god; respectful address to a man

sandhosham
>happiness

thamboolam
>a gift to mark an auspicious occassion; wedding favour

thaali
>sacred thread tied around the neck at the moment of marriage

thambi
>literally, younger brother; can be used to address any younger man

thappu
>a circular frame drum made with cow skin

thinnai
>a raised platform outside the entryway of a house

thavil
>a large two-headed drum, traditionally played at weddings

upma
>a breakfast dish

vaadhyar
>teacher; "vaadhyare" is used to address such a person

vaale
>come! (colloquial)

vaanga
>please come (formal welcome)

vanakkam
>greetings, welcome

veshti
>lower-body garment worn by men

vibuthi
>sacred ash

About the Author

Indra Soundar Rajan, born in 1958, has been one of the best-selling Tamil popular novelists for more than three decades. He is the author of hundreds of novels and short stories, some of which have been published in English translation in *The Blaft Anthology of Tamil Pulp Fiction*. He is also well-known for his television screenplays, such as the hit megaserials *Marmadesam*, *Sivamayam*, and *Rudraveena*. He lives in Madurai.

About the Translator

Nirmal works in construction and runs a data management startup. He has previously translated stories for *The Blaft Anthology of Tamil Pulp Fiction, Vol 3*. He lives in Chennai with his wife and four dogs.

www.ingramcontent.com/pod-product-compliance
Lightning Source LLC
LaVergne TN
LVHW040014200726
843493LV00005B/1266